A Texan's Touch

WHISPERING SPRINGS, TEXAS
BOOK TEN

CYNTHIA D'ALBA

Riante Romance

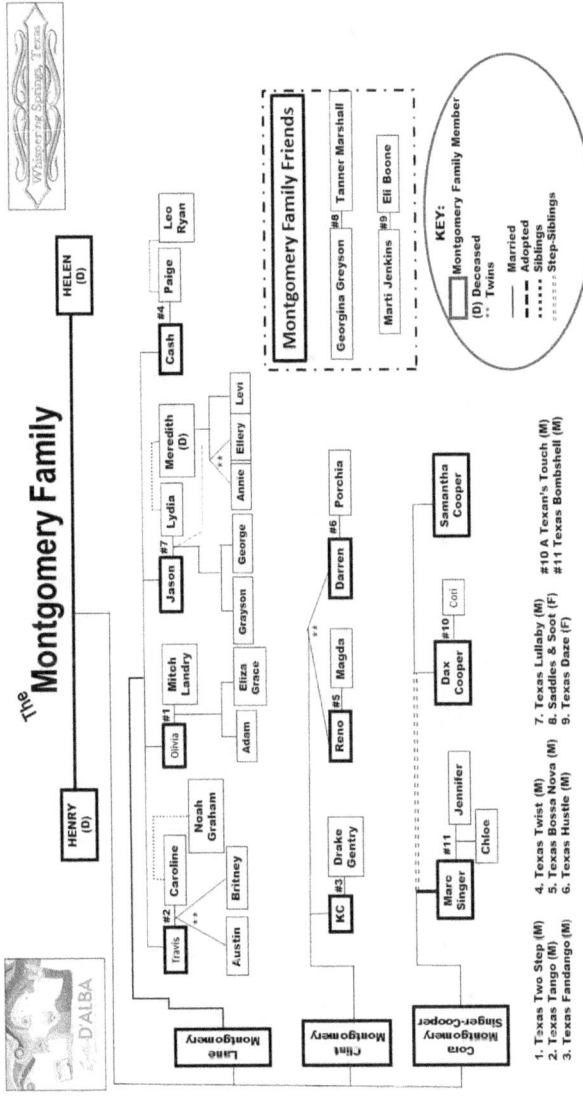

The Montgomery Family

Whispering Springs, Texas

D'ALBA

HENRY (D) — HELEN (D)

KEY:
- [ ] Montgomery Family Member
- (D) Deceased
- ** Twins
- ── Married
- ━━ Adopted
- ▬▬ Siblings
- ········ Step-Siblings

Montgomery Family Friends

Georgina Greyson #8 Tanner Marshall

Marti Jenkins #9 Eli Boone

Lanie Montgomery

Clint Montgomery

Cora Montgomery Singer-Cooper

Travis #2 — Caroline — Noah Graham
Austin, Britney

Olivia — Mitch Landry #1
Eliza Grace, Adam, Grayson

Jason #7 — Lydia — Meredith (D)
George, Annie **, Ellery, Levi

Cash #4 — Paige
Leo, Ryan

Drake Gentry

KC #3

Marc Singer #11 — Jennifer
Chloe

Reno #5 — Magda

Darren #6 — Porchia

Dax Cooper #10 — Cori — Samantha Cooper

1. Texas Two Step (M)
2. Texas Tango (M)
3. Texas Fandango (M)
4. Texas Twist (M)
5. Texas Bossa Nova (M)
6. Texas Hustle (M)
7. Texas Lullaby (M)
8. Saddles & Scoot (F)
9. Texas Daze (F)
10. A Texan's Touch (M)
11. Texas Bombshell (M)

For Shane Rice and Kobi

#10yearchallenge

Copyright

Cover Artist: Elle James
Editor: Delilah Devlin
Cover Models: Shane Rice & Kobi
Cover Photo by Tom Tyson

One

The parched dirt soaked up his blood as fast as it poured from his body. Army Major Daxton Cooper had no choice but to accept his reality. With multiple bullet wounds and his fucking leg blown to hell, he was going to die in this God-forsaken place. His last goddamn day in Afghanistan would be his last day on Earth. He was sure that day had to be the worst day of his life.

He'd been wrong.

The months of multiple surgeries and recovery, followed by grueling physical therapy had provided him with five hundred and fifty days of the worst days in his life.

Impossible to believe, but his mother had just added another day to his list of worst days in his life.

Dax watched his brother sign another piece of paper, flip it over, and begin reading another report that had to be approved.

"Let me ask you something," Dax muttered. "It's

1

probably still against the law to put a hit out on Mom, right?"

His brother, Marc Singer, set his pen on the desk and looked up. "As the sheriff of Whispering Springs County, I can say with definite authority that you cannot put a hit out on Mom. What'd she do this time?"

Dax dragged his fingers through his hair. "She arranged a blind date for me."

Marc shrugged and went back to his reports. "So, tell her no."

"I tried to, but...." he shook his head, "I owe her. For the past year, she put her life on hold to help me."

"So, go."

"Wow. Thanks for the excellent advice."

Marc looked up and pointed his pen across the desk at Dax. "Look, *Major*, you're a grown man. Go or don't go, but don't sit here whining about Mom. Besides,

what do you want me to say? It's one freaking date. Go, have dinner, come home. Obligation done. Easy."

"Hell, you're older than me and single. She ever set you up on a blind date?"

"God, no." Marc shivered dramatically.

"Why not?"

Marc looked down at the stack of papers on his desk and shrugged. "No idea."

Dax knew his brother well enough to recognize bullshit when he heard it, but he decided to let it slide for now.

The sheriff leaned back in this chair with a frown. "Now that you mention it, I am a little surprised."

"That she hasn't set up on a date or that she set me up on one?"

"Both, actually. Plus, how does she know anyone in Dallas to fix you up with? She's lived in Maine, for what? The last forty years?"

"Not Dallas. The woman lives here in Whispering Springs."

"What? That's crazy. Um, what have you told her about me?"

Dax gave his brother a disgusted look. "Nothing. Apparently, you've done a great job lying to Mom for the past decade. As far as I know, she doesn't know you live in her old hometown, if that's what has you worried."

"I'm not worried. Whispering Springs is simply where my job is located. My being here has nothing to do with Mom growing up here."

"Right. Keep telling yourself that. And that's why you have a post office box in Dallas, right? To keep her from worrying?" Dax snorted. "You're such a liar. If she wanted to, Mom could break you in five minutes."

"I suspect she knows anyway. As you say, she's smart but stick to the subject. Why a blind date, and why here in Whispering Springs?

"She thinks I'm in Dallas with you, and apparently, driving to Whispering Springs for a date is doable, so she set me up."

"True." Marc lifted his hands palms up and then gestured for him to go on.

Dax sighed loudly. "Seems she met this woman's mom on Facebook, and they hit it off since she lives in Whispering Springs. It was probably a way for Mom to keep up with what's going on in her old hometown without having to actually talk to her brothers."

"Still, a blind date? What was she thinking?"

Dax felt the flush as it climbed up his neck. "Fuck," he muttered under his breath.

Marc looked puzzled. "What?"

"It's a fucking pity date," Dax snapped. "Can't you see that? She figured no one would go out with a cripple. So, make 'em go on a blind date, and they don't know until they get there."

"What in the hell are you talking about?"

"Me!" He jerked up his pant leg until his artificial left leg was exposed. "Remember this? And if that isn't bad enough, my face has hideous scars from the shrapnel, and my chest and arms have scars. I look like Frankenstein's monster. Of course, no woman would want to date me."

Marc stared; his mouth slightly agape. "You're crazy. You're a war hero."

Dax waved his hand across his face and down his body. "Take a peek. It's not pretty. On second thought, don't take a peek."

"Now, you're being stupid. Those few places on your face are nothing—barely visible. Besides, any woman who would judge you on looks isn't worth knowing."

"Don't kid yourself, bro. Women can be as bad as men about how someone looks." He shook his head. "Doesn't matter. I owe Mom, so I'll go on this damned date, provided the poor woman doesn't walk out as soon as she meets me."

"What's her name?"

"Last name's Lambert. Ring any bells for you?"

"Pretty common name. Only Lamberts I know are Clover Jean and Dale Lambert." Marc's eyebrows arched. "They've got three daughters. Might be one of them. Got a first name?"

Dax pulled out his cell phone and opened the calendar. "Um, Cori Lambert."

Marc nodded. "Cora Belle Lambert. I know her. Nice girl, but..."

"But what?"

"She's a really nice person. Not a looker like her older sister, Elsie Belle. Now that one's a total knock-out. She's a former Miss Texas and a runner up to Miss America, but she's got a soul as black as coal."

"What do you mean, not a looker? Are you saying she's so ugly that she'd appreciate a date with anyone, even someone like me? Good God." He dragged his fingers through his hair again. "How pitiful is this? Our two mothers think their own children are so unappealing to the other sex that they're trying to put the two uglies together."

Marc groaned. "For God's sake, she's not ugly, and you're not so hideous that you'd scare children."

"Gee, thanks. Asshole."

Marc grinned. "Really, the only thing I worry about is that she's so much smarter than you."

"Har-har. And how do you know she's smarter?"

"Because she's *Doctor* Cora Belle Lambert. She's a psychologist here in town. Actually, I do know her. Not well, but she seems like a nice woman."

Dax leaned forward. "Do you think Mom thinks I need psychological help, and that's what this is all about?"

A loud guffaw burst from Marc. "No. So, when's the big night?"

"Tomorrow," he said glumly. "We're supposed to meet at Rick's on the River. Know it?"

Nodding, Marc said, "Yep. Nice place. Get a table outside by the river if possible. Inside is okay. It's just nicer on the patio. Good food." He eyed Dax's worn jeans and the T-shirt with a hole under the arm. "However, I'd suggest something other than what you're wearing."

"Thanks for the fashion advice." Dax struggled onto his feet, his fucking left leg still wanting to give him a fit. He balanced on his cane. "So, Mom really hasn't ever tried to set you up on some blind date?"

Marc wouldn't meet Dax's eyes. "Shit," he muttered under his breath. "Fine. She did try a couple of times."

"So, what happened?"

"Told her I was seeing someone."

"Hmm. So, you lied."

His brother shrugged. "You don't know that. Maybe I am."

Dax scoffed. "Right."

Marc pointed toward the door. "Go. Git gone. I've got work to do. See you at home."

As ordered, Dax stood, gave his brother a one-finger salute, and walked out of the office. Today was much like the life ahead of him—no plans for either.

His original life plan had been military to retirement, maybe around age fifty. However, at the ripe old age of thirty-four, an improvised explosive device, aka IED, had changed everything about who he was and what he would do with his life.

The IED had blown off his left leg from mid-calf down, fractured the tibia and fibula of his right leg, and had given him third-degree burns on both arms and shoulders and second-degree burns on his neck and face, not to mention the various cuts and abrasions all over his body. If not for the quick action of his team and the incredible medical care he'd received, he'd be dead.

Sometimes, he wondered if everyone wouldn't have been better off if he'd died over there.

He'd ended up in Texas near his brother because, frankly, he had nowhere he had to be and nowhere he wanted to go. He'd already been to Maine and stayed with his parents for a while, but his mother had smothered him as only a loving mother could. And even though she hadn't meant to make him feel helpless, all her fawning had produced that exact feeling.

Now that he was in Texas, he had to keep up the

required daily physical therapy for the loss of muscle mass in his left leg. The VA had hooked him up with a local physical therapist. He'd crossed his fingers for a sexy woman to put him through his daily paces. No such luck. He'd ended up with a two-hundred and fifty-pound ex-Dallas Cowboy linebacker who, while thankful for Dax's service, wasn't at all intimated by Dax's military persona or the severity of his injuries. The damn man worked Dax like he was in a second round of boot camp. Sweat, grunts, and pain accompanied every session, but Dax could see the progress, which only drove him to work harder.

Until he had some idea of where he wanted to land and how to spend the next fifty or so years, Dax kept possessions minimal. Everything he owned could be packed in a duffle bag. He'd given thought to buying a new car or truck, something slick and flashy with automatic everything, but his ambiguity about the future held him back.

He headed out of the Sheriff's Department toward the truck Marc had loaned him. Damn thing was a stick, so it just about killed him to shift gears. His masochistic physical therapist loved that he was forced to run through gears. He'd assured Dax that the manual drive truck would be a good exercise to build strength in his left leg and stretch the burned areas of his arms.

Dax pointed the truck out of town. He'd been in town about a month, and most of his time had been spent settling in, sleeping—as much as a man who had nightmares could—and getting set up for his daily physical therapy sessions. But in the down-times, or when his brain wouldn't stop sending pictures of blood and body parts, he'd taken to exploring as a means to distraction. First, he'd been in all the local shops in Whispering Springs, and now he felt the call to drive further out on rural county roads.

Until now, he'd never been to Texas. He and Marc had talked about the state and his brother's adopted town, but like most people, he'd never realized just how huge the state was nor how unique the different regions could be. Texas could be a country unto itself.

Dust rolled behind him as he took the twists and turns in the roads. Alongside the gravel and dirt lanes were thousands of acres of rolling hills, forests, ponds, and rivers. In the years since Marc relocated to Whispering Springs, he had sent pictures of the area, but they hadn't begun to capture the lushness of the terrain.

A field where a herd of fat cattle grazing on waving green stalks of grass caught his attention. He pulled off the road and rolled down his window. Calves hung close to their mothers, bleating for milk, and moving with their mommas when they moved to a fresh grassy area. Overhead, birds flew and cawed, flittering from tree to tree.

A sense of peace quieted areas inside Dax hadn't realized were noisy. He settled heavily in the seat with a long sigh. He had no idea how long he sat and soaked in the area's beauty, nor how long he might have remained if the sound of thudding horse hooves hadn't broken the serenity.

A muscular man on a large, chestnut horse reined to a stop inside the fenced yard beside the truck. He clicked his tongue and brought the still-dancing horse to a stand. With a thumb, he pushed his cowboy hat back a little, then crossed his forearms on the saddle's horn.

"Howdy," he said in a friendly tone, but caution flared on his face. "You lost?"

"No, sorry. Daydreaming. Saw your fields and stopped for a minute to enjoy the view."

"Actually, you've been parked here for almost twenty minutes. Thought maybe you were having a problem with your truck."

Dax shook his head. "Sorry," he repeated and turned the ignition key. The engine whined and groaned before it finally fired.

The man frowned. "I know that truck." Now, his eyes narrowed in heavy suspicion. "Who are you? Where'd you get that truck?"

"Whoa. Hold on, cowboy. I'm Dax Cooper. The truck belongs to my brother, Sheriff Marc Singer."

His comment didn't appear to soothe the wary cowboy.

"Really? Singer? Cooper?" The man pulled a phone from his pocket. "Why don't you wait right here while I call the sheriff?"

"Sure. Whatever."

Dax cut off the engine, blew out a long breath, and settled back against the seat. He hoped his brother hadn't left the office. Damn cowboy might pull a gun on him while imagining himself as Deputy Barney Fife.

"Hey, Sara. Travis Montgomery. Fine. Fine. Thank you. Is Marc in? Can I talk to him?"

Well, well. Cousin Travis. Wasn't this interesting?

"Marc. Travis Montgomery." He laughed. "Right. Anyway, I found this guy driving your truck out by my place. Says name is Dax Cooper. You know him?" There was a long pause. "You don't say." Travis leaned over until he could see into the truck's window. "Nope. Can't say he looks like you at all." He laughed again. "Right." He looked at Dax. "Says he got all the good genes. You're a pool of bad genes."

Dax rolled his eye. "Tell him to kiss my ass."

Travis chuckled. "You were right. Kiss your ass. Right. Okay. Thanks." He slipped the phone back into his pocket. "Sorry. We've had a little trouble out here lately with some cattle rustling."

"No kidding? I guess I didn't realize things like that still go on."

Travis answered with a scoff. "You better believe it. The stories I could tell you. I'm getting ready to head up to the house. You want to come up? I'm sure there's fresh iced tea."

"Thanks. Another time. I'm just trying to get the lay of the land."

"You moving to this area?"

Dax shrugged. "Not sure." He looked around. "But it is some beautiful territory."

"That it is." Travis pointed down the road. "If

you stay on this road about seven miles or so, you'll hit Rutherford Road. Take a right and follow that road for about twenty miles, and you'll hit the highway back into Whispering Springs. From there, you probably know your way."

"Appreciate it. Wasn't sure if I'd have to backtrack to find my way back to town."

"I'll have Caroline, that's my wife, get in touch and have you guys out for dinner this week. Wait. You married? I can have Caroline call your wife directly."

"Nope. No wife. No girlfriend. And before you ask, no boyfriend either."

Travis grinned. "Whatever flips your skirt, man."

Dax chuckled. "I'm sure dinner would be great. Thanks."

Travis touched the brim of his hat, turned the stallion around and rode away. Dax pulled away, a smile twitching on his lips. His brother, Marc Montgomery Singer, had had years to get to know his uncles and cousins, not that they knew Marc was a relative. His brother had kept that tidbit under his hat.

Now it was Dax's turn to meet his extended family. He'd be having dinner with Travis and his family with or without his brother.

And he just might tell them his full name, Daxton Montgomery Cooper.

Wouldn't that be a shocker for everybody?

Cori Lambert chewed the cuticle on her thumb while listening to her mother on the phone. She pulled her thumb away and looked at the red skin with disgust. Chomping on her cuticles was such a bad habit, but it was impossible to stop, especially when she was stressed and frustrated, like now.

"Are you listening Cora Belle? You have to be at Rick's on the River at six tomorrow night."

"I heard you, but good God, Momma. I can get my own dates."

"I know that, honey, but you know how close I am with his mother."

"So, you've said, but really? Someone from Facebook has a son in the area, and you think I should go on a date with him? For all you know, he could be a serial killer, or a rapist, or worse—boring."

"Don't take that tone with me, little lady. He just retired from the military, so you know he's a good man."

"Right," Cori said. "Like rape and murder never happen in the military."

Her mother sighed. "Just do this one thing for me. I promise I'll never ask a favor of you again."

Cori scoffed. "You will too."

"I'm just worried about you, honey. I want you to find a good man like your sister has."

In that case, she'd need body sculpting, a new face, bleach for her hair, contacts to change her eye color, and a new personality. No problem.

"This is the last time, Momma. I mean it. Next time, I won't show up, and you'll be embarrassed.

And, let me add, I don't need a man. I'm happy with my life. I'm happy in my job. Stop fretting over my love life."

Very little of what she'd just said was true, but that was Cori's business, not her mother's.

"It's a mother's job to worry about her daughter," Clover Jean Lambert said.

Cori sighed. "You've got another daughter, you know."

"Yes, yes, but Annabelle is too young to be thinking of marriage and babies. She has years of college before then. You, on the other hand, are at a perfect age."

Right. Thirty-three was the perfect age. Her mother would never give up.

"I've got to run. I've got a patient in five minutes."

"Call me on Saturday, and let me know how the date went."

Cori rolled her eyes, even though her mother couldn't see it.

"And don't roll your eyes," Clover Jean said.

Cori glanced around the office. "Crap, Momma. You have a camera in my office or something?"

"We'll just call it an *or something*. Love you."

After Cori dropped her cell into her purse, she shook her head with a laugh. She did love her mother. She meant well, but...

The phone on her desk rang. "Yes?"

"Dr. Lambert. Jack Rhett is here."

"Send him in."

She pulled out her folder for Jack Rhett. Sixteen years old. Three school fights. A couple of school suspensions. A foster child lost in the system since his mother had gone to prison for killing his father when Jack had been nine. In two more years, he'd be out on his own, and unfortunately, he was nowhere near ready for adulthood.

Her door opened.

"Hi, Jack. Come on in and have a seat."

A lanky teenager with dirty, long, black hair shuffled into her office and dropped heavily into the chair. He slid down until his ass was barely touching the seat's material.

"So, Jack," Cori stated. "Let's talk about what's going on with you?"

"Nothing."

"I see," she said with a nod. "How are things at your foster parents' house?"

His mouth twisted into a snarl. "Amos is an asshole."

Amos and Lillian Vander were new to the foster system and had taken in Jack when he was fifteen. During his last appointment, Jack had mentioned that the Vanders had taken in a five-year-old girl to foster temporarily.

"You've mentioned that before. Is there something specific that he's done that we need to talk about?"

Jack shook his head.

"How's the new child doing? I can't remember her name, or did you tell me?"

"Sally. Her name is Sally. She cries all the time."

"It must be hard."

He shrugged. "I'll be out of there soon enough."

"And then what?"

"Doesn't matter," he said with another shrug. "Life sucks."

Two

A t five a.m., Dax walked into the kitchen and
hung his cane on the back of a chair before
pouring himself a cup of coffee.

"I hate you," Marc said.

Dax frowned. "Why? What did I do?"

Marc indicated Dax's clothes. "You're up,
dressed, and awake. I can barely hold my eyes open."

"Training. You're getting soft in your old age."

"Bite me," Marc said with a chuckle and then his
face grew serious. "I hate to be all big brother in your
shit, but are you okay? I heard you roaming the house
last night."

With a shrug, Dax sat. "Sorry I bothered you."

"Never said that you did. Just said I heard you.
Having trouble sleeping again?"

"Not again. Still."

Marc sat quietly as Dax sipped his coffee.

"It's like, whenever I close my eyes, I see all the
smoke and my blood." Dax paused and swallowed

against the anger that he fought to control. "I hear my guys screaming, others crying. Around me, bullets ping off rocks and metal."

Marc remained quiet.

"Fuck," Dax muttered under his breath. His fingers gripped his coffee mug tight. His knuckles whitened from the pressure. He hated feeling helpless against his nightmares. *Hated it*. Hell, he hated the word *helpless*. He should be able to control these dreams. They were just dreams, for God's sake. He simply needed to get control of his mind.

"Give it time," Marc said. "Give yourself some time. Pace around the house all you want."

"If I'm in your way, I can move on, man."

"Don't be an idiot. If I didn't want you here, I'd have locked the door when I heard you were coming."

Dax smiled. "Asshole."

Marc grinned. "Yeah, and don't you forget it. I wanted to talk to you about running into Travis yesterday, but by the time I got home from that arson fire, I was brain-dead. What the hell were you doing at Halo M ranch?"

Dax appreciated Marc's change of subject. He knew his brother was trying to help, and right now, he'd rather have Marc ragging on him than feeling sorry for him.

"Total fluke. I was driving around and stumbled upon his ranch."

"Are you sure you didn't go there deliberately? Don't fuck up everything I've worked for."

"Screw you. It was a fluke that I ended up there, and a fluke he happened to be close to the road. Besides, he invited us to dinner, and I accepted."

Before Marc could reply, there was a loud banging on his front door, much like Dax used to do when he wanted to get his guys up after a night of heavy partying.

Marc shoved his chair back to stand. His robe flapped open, exposing his white undershirt and briefs.

"Want me to get it?" Dax asked. "At least I'm dressed."

"Keep your seat. I can get it." He pulled his robe around him but there was no belt to cinch it closed.

"I might limp a little, but I can answer a damned door." Dax whipped out of his chair and whirled around to prove his point. He wobbled from the quick spin, but caught his balance at the last minute. He headed for the front door with a determined stride, albeit one that was a little uneven. He flung it open, prepared to defend himself, if necessary, but he wasn't ready for the attack that came. Opening his mouth to speak, nothing came out. Then he wrapped his arms around his baby sister. Her long dark hair clung to his morning beard like Velcro.

"Sami," Dax said as he hugged her tight. "God, I've missed you."

"Who is it?" Marc called from the kitchen.

Dax lifted Sami Cooper off her feet in a tight bear hug. "I can't believe you're here." He kissed her cheek, now salty with her shed tears. "How did you know I was here?"

The scratch of a chair being shoved back resounded in the house. "Who's here? Dax?"

Sami was jerked from Dax's arms as Marc pulled her into an embrace. "My God, Sami. Where did you come from?"

Samantha Montgomery Cooper laughed as she stepped from Marc's arms. "Well, hell, guys, if I'd known you'd be so glad to see me, I'd have come visit before now."

Dax leaned back and studied her. "Damn, you look great. How are you?"

She sighed. "I need coffee in the worst way. Black and strong."

"Gotcha covered," Marc said. "Come on back to the kitchen."

Sami put an arm around the shoulders of each brother, and the three siblings staggered into the kitchen, Dax's limp becoming more pronounced with each step. He fucking hated his left leg. Still, he hid the pain and joined into the gaiety of the moment, as much as any man in throbbing pain could. Sounds of laughter and the mixture of three voices talking over each other bounced off walls that were used to quiet.

After each of them had fresh coffee and found seats at the table, Marc said, "You've got some 'splaining to do, little sister. What are you doing here, and how in the hell did you find me? My address isn't exactly well known, at least within the family."

"If I tell you how I found you, I'd have to kill you."

Marc rolled his eyes.

Dax put his arm around Sami. "I don't care how she found you." He squeezed her shoulders. "I am so glad to see you."

"I've been worried about you," she said. "How are you doing? I mean, *really* doing? Don't give me the same *I'm fine* story that you bullshit me with every time I call."

Dax grimaced. "So, you've talked to Mom?"

"Yeah."

He shifted, moving his left leg into a more comfortable position. "I'm okay."

When she quirked the corner of her mouth and rolled her eyes, he sighed. "The knee's doing great. The left leg still wants to give me trouble, so I'm still doing PT. I've some scars from the burns, but those will get better with time, or so I'm told." He squeezed her shoulder again. "I am so glad to see you. It's been, what? A year?"

Nodding, she said, "Pretty much. Saw you in Germany before you were shipped out to the States. Of course, you were drugged out of your mind, so I'm not sure you remember. Do you?"

"Not really, but kind of. It's like a really nice dream. Enough about my crappy body, let's hear about you."

"Spill it, you little monster," Marc said.

Dax grinned at Marc's use of Sami's nickname.

"I've got so much to tell you guys." She blew out

21

a long sigh. "But I'm exhausted. I just drove into town."

"From where?" Marc asked with a frown.

"Maine."

"What? Are you nuts? That's like a three-day drive."

"I know. I know. But I wanted to bring my car. And I wanted to bring Mike with me. I took it slow, so cool your jets."

"Mike?" both men said at the same time.

She grinned. "My dog. The most faithful male I've ever lived with."

"Where is he?" Marc asked.

"I left him in the car until I knew if I could bring him in."

"I let your brother in. Mike can't be worse."

Sami laughed.

Dax threw a dishtowel across the table at Marc.

"I'll go get him." She hurried from the kitchen.

"Can't believe she's here," Dax said.

"I wonder what she wants," Marc answered. "You know Sami. She wants something,"

Dax nodded as he drank his coffee.

The front door slammed, and nails scratched on the hardwood floor as Sami led the ugliest mutt Max had ever seen into the kitchen.

"Meet Mike." Sami's face was lit with excitement.

Marc held out a hand to let the dog sniff it before stroking Mike's head.

"Where'd you come from?" he directed to the dog.

"Iraq," Sami answered. "He showed up one night, moved in, and stayed. I couldn't leave him behind." She knelt and wrapped her arms around his neck. "I love him so much."

The two men exchanged glances.

"He's a good-looking guy," Dax lied.

"I know," she said, kissing the dog's forehead. "He's a good boy, aren't you, Mike?"

"Let's get back to you being in Texas. The only way you can be here at this hour of the morning is if you drove all night." Dax crossed his arm. "I know you're smarter than that."

She yawned. "I stopped in Memphis, caught a little shut-eye, and moved on. The traffic is so much better at night. Plus..." She danced a little jig. "I couldn't wait to get to my brothers."

"Shit," Marc muttered.

"What?" she asked with a frown. "You don't want me to visit?"

"No, of course not. I love having my baby sister here, but look around. Me, Dax, and now, you. There's no way Mom won't be close on your heels."

"She can't get away for the next three months, so we're safe," Sami said. "She's teaching an advanced class in abstract algebra all summer, so she has to stay in Maine."

"You're here for the summer?" Marc asked. "Last I checked, you and the Army were having an affair."

"I'm out. Did my time and didn't re-up."

"So, what now?" Dax asked.

She shrugged. "I thought maybe you had a place

23

for another deputy. I mean, I was a damned fine MP."

"I'm pretty sure working for Marc is a horrible idea," Dax said. "You two would kill each other within a month."

"Two weeks, tops," Marc replied. "Sorry, sis, but no."

"You're telling me that if someone walked in with my education and experience, you wouldn't hire them on the spot?"

Marc took a sip of coffee. "If I had an opening, I probably would, but not you. Historically, this department had some trouble with nepotism, and it caused all kinds of problems, so I'm not going there."

She blew out a dejected sigh. "I understand, I do, but police work is all I know."

"You don't have to live here," Marc said. "Why not go back to Maine? Closer to the folks? I'm sure Mom would love that."

She frowned. "You trying to get rid of me?"

"Of course not. But all of us here in one spot? Well, I'm not sure it's a good idea."

"He's worried about you and me blowing our family relationship cover," Dax said.

"That is so stupid. Why didn't you just tell everyone that Cora Montgomery is your mother and the sister of Lane and Clint Montgomery?"

Marc's eyes closed momentarily as he shook his head. "I don't know. I really don't. I didn't mean to stay this long. I was going to drop in for a few months, check out the branch of the family we didn't know, and move on." He took a big gulp of coffee. "Dominos began falling, and I found myself running for sheriff and loving the job. I don't want to leave. But trust me when I say, the Montgomerys have the ability to pull the rug out from under me and run me out of town. I've been walking on eggshells every day just waiting for the ax to fall."

"That's no way to live," Dax said.

"I know," Marc agreed. "I'm glad you're both here, but settling here? You might want to think long and hard about that."

"Well," Sami said on a puff of air. "I believe I'll start my stay in Whispering Springs with some sleep. You got an extra bedroom, Marc?"

"Sure. You'll find a couple of unmade beds--"

Dax cleared his throat and arched a brow. "Excuse me?"

Marc laughed. "Fine. Mine's unmade. Brother Perfect has made his."

Dax stood. "Come on, Sami. I'll show you which room I'm using. I'm sure Marc needs to get to work."

Marc glanced toward the clock on the microwave. "Crap." He gulped down the last of his coffee. "I need to get dressed." He stood and kissed his sister on the cheek. "I'm glad you're here. Let me think about your employment problem." He started to leave the room, but stopped and turned back. "With all three of us here, we need groceries."

"Got it covered," Dax said. "I'll go."

"Thanks."

"You look like you're going to faceplant on Marc's nice wooden table," Dax said to Sami.

Sami staggered a little as she stood. "I think you're right." She hugged him tight. "I am so glad you're okay. The last time I saw you, you looked pretty much like death warmed over."

"I'm fine. Let's worry about getting you settled."

"Sounds like a plan."

Within an hour, Marc was gone, and Sami was asleep, leaving Dax alone with his thoughts, which wasn't always a good thing.

Dr. Cori Lambert shut down her computer for the day. Leaving at one in the afternoon felt so decadent, especially since she heading to a spa. Most days, including Fridays, she was lucky to be home by seven. Heavens knew if she didn't grocery shop this after-noon, she'd be eating ice cubes and drinking water tomorrow. Maybe having a dinner date tonight wasn't the worst thing for a woman who hated grocery shopping as much as she did.

She pulled her purse from a lower desk drawer and walked into the reception area.

"I'm gone," she said to her receptionist, Merlene.

Merlene looked at her watch, and then gave Cori an arched eyebrow. "Got some primping to do before tonight's hot date?"

Cori laughed. "More like I have to hit Nelson's market on the way home. No food in the house."

"And?"

"Okay, fine. I'm getting a mani-pedi too."

Her receptionist laughed. "You deserve it. Hope your date rocks."

"I just hope he's not a serial killer."

When Cori had scheduled her manicure and pedicure appointments, she'd made them for early afternoon, figuring she would have time to hit Nelson's, take the refrigerated foodstuff home, and still have plenty of time left to get ready. She hadn't counted on her nail technician's prolonged telephone calls or the constant interruptions in the salon. By the time she parked at Nelson's Neighborhood Market, all her plans of a leisurely walk through the store were shot. She had thirty minutes tops to grab what she needed, pay, and race home. Otherwise, she'd be more than fashionably late to Rick's on the River.

She saved the dairy for last, which was, of course, in the far back corner. She raced her cart down aisle fourteen and crashed into another buggy as she whipped around the corner.

"I am so sorry," she said, glancing up into the most incredible set of azure eyes.

"No problem," the man pushing the cart said. "I wasn't looking where I was going."

He gestured for her to proceed around him, which was the last thing she wanted. When he smiled, the creases in the corners of his eyes deepened, and a pair of deep dimples drilled into his cheeks. All her female parts sat up to take notice. The chiseled chin with the various grooves and lines on his face spoke of a life in the sun. The twinkle in his eyes said he had a million stories, and she found she wanted to hear each one in detail.

She had never picked up a guy at a grocery store. Had never met anyone she wanted to pick up, and now that she had, she had absolutely no time to do so, not that she had any idea how to pick up guys. Now, if she were her sister Elsie Belle, men would be following her all over the store trying to pick her up. Alas, Cori wasn't a candidate for Miss Texas and would never be.

"Sorry again," she said, swinging her cart around his and pushing it toward the eggs and milk. This time, the *sorry* wasn't about running into his cart. It was about her lack of time to explore what could have been.

One quick glance over her shoulder told her he apparently hadn't been as mesmerized as she. He was long gone. She sighed and set a dozen eggs in her basket. She did have the utmost worst luck when it came to meeting new men.

Wheeling to the front of the store, she miraculously found an empty checkout lane. Minutes later, she was headed for her car so she could rush home to get ready for a mystery date that she had no interest in.

Man, life sucked sometimes.

At a little before six, Cori pulled into the lot at Rick's on the River. She and her date, Dax Cooper, had sent texts back and forth, but she had no idea what he looked like. The reservation was under his name, so at least they would be able to connect.

After touching up her lipstick in the mirror and fussing with her hair, which absolutely refused to stay the least bit curled, she slid out and locked her car. Her hands shook a little. The closer she'd gotten to the restaurant, the more her heart had picked up the pace. Thank goodness it wasn't summer in Texas or else she'd be battling sweat rings under her arms... from the heat and her nerves.

This was her last blind date, and she meant it. She knew her mother loved her as much as she loved her other two daughters. It was just that her sisters, Elsie and Anna, favored their mother. Beautiful, natural blondes with jade-green eyes and bodies that refused to store even an ounce of fat. The kind of women who never needed a blind date. The kind of women you never introduced to your boyfriend because you knew he would fall immediately for your sister and dump you for her. Cori knew that from experience.

Unfortunately, Cori took after her paternal grandmother, a lovely woman known for her brilliant mind rather than her brilliant body. Cori had inherited her Grandma Lambert's blah-brown hair and brown eyes as well as her life-long weight battle. Even now, Cori couldn't get into a size ten pair of jeans if her life depended on it. And let's not even begin to talk about the definition of a muffin top.

As she walked past the landscaped bushes that separated the dining patio from the parking lot, she glanced over, and her heart flipped. The man from today's grocery cart crash sat alone at a table. She ducked behind a tall plant. What was he doing here?

Leaning forward, she peeked around the greenery. He lifted a glass of iced tea to his mouth. As he set the glass back on the table, his head turned in her direction. She snapped back before she could be seen.

Thank you, fate. Now, if she could only gather the courage to act. Her brain went into overdrive with different scenarios of how to "accidentally" cross his path again.

As subtly as possible, she ventured a glimpse between the thick bushes. As before, he was still alone. There was an extra place setting at his table, but it was possible that the extra setting could have been there when he'd sat down, and the hostess had failed to remove it.

Grocery Man checked his watch. Damn. That reminded her that she had a date waiting inside for her. In the last exchange of text messages, her date had suggested they eat inside because of the slight chance of rain. She'd had no problem with that suggestion. Her hair hated humidity.

What she would do is meet her date, explain that she'd been fighting a migraine all day, and ask to reschedule. She'd get back into her car, drive out, and circle the block. If her date's car was gone—she'd have to make sure to find out what he was driving— she'd go back in and accidentally cross paths with Grocery Man.

She had never done anything like this. Nervous tension twisted her insides, but she'd missed her chance this afternoon. She wasn't going to let him slip through her fingers again. With a plan firm in her mind and nerves making her knees shake, she entered Rick's on the River and gave the hostess Dax Cooper's name.

The hostess led her through the interior and out on the patio. When she stopped beside a table, Cori's mouth dropped slightly as she stared into Grocery Man's startling blue eyes.

Three

If there was one thing that Dax hated, it was people who were late. If he made an appointment, he expected the other person to be there on time. There hadn't been a man or woman in his command who hadn't understood that expectation and respected it.

He checked his cell phone. This supposedly brilliant woman was seven minutes late. How long should he wait? He didn't want to be here anyway. Fifteen more minutes, and he was gone.

He was reading the menu for the third time when he caught movement out of the corner of his eye. His heart slowed. His breathing deepened. Muscles in his arms and shoulders tightened, ready to fend off an attack.

"Here he is," the restaurant hostess said as she stepped up alongside the table.

He relaxed his on-guard alert, but nonetheless

braced himself for the rejection he was sure was coming.

Before the IED, he'd been a decent-looking guy, or so the women he'd known had told him. They'd cooed over his eyes. Caressed his cheeks. Kissed his lips.

But since that horrible day, he didn't look like Daxton Cooper. Lines and scars marred his left cheek and neck. His mouth pulled on the left side. The skin on his chest and arms was taut and stretched from the scarring.

He'd found that a man's appearance was vital to attracting a woman, and he, unfortunately, was far from handsome these days.

Taking a steadying breath, he raised his head to see his date, waiting for the polite "I am so sorry. I have a migraine" excuse he'd heard before. Instead, he felt a jab like a good right hook to his jaw.

He stood, his thigh bumping the edge of the table and rattling all the flatware. To his shock, and utter delight, the beautiful woman from the grocery store stood beside his table, wearing a quizzical expression. The stunning woman he'd walked up and down aisles looking for was here. The one who had smiled at him so brightly. She'd been on his mind all afternoon, so much so that he's already decided to hit Nelson's Market next Friday in hopes of their paths crossing again.

"Grocery man," she said.

"Cart crasher," he replied with a smile.

Her responding smile lit up her face. "You're Dax Cooper?"

"That would be me," he said with a nod.

The hostess pulled out Cori's chair and she sat. Once Cori had the leather-bound menu in her hand, the hostess left.

"Well," she said, "this is a surprise."

His hope deflated like a popped balloon. Was he a good surprise or a bad surprise? "I hope this is a good surprise."

She smiled, and his insides warmed at the vision. "Very much so."

Her shiny, auburn hair caught the candlelight from the table lamp. Depending on how she moved her head, strands of red, burgundy, or chestnut would shine. Her chocolate eyes sparkled. Her lips were like strawberries in their prime, full and luscious.

"So, no whiplash from today? No long-term injuries?" she asked with a saucy grin.

He chuckled. "No. I seem to have weathered the accident without needing medical care."

"Would you like to start off your dinner with a drink from our bar?"

Dax and Cori looked at the young waiter standing there. Dax wondered how long he'd been trying to get their attention.

Cori eyed his iced tea.

He lifted it and said, "Feel free to order a drink. I'm on a medication that doesn't mix well with alcohol."

"Great. It's been one of those weeks. I'll have a merlot."

The waiter nodded. "We have a few specials tonight if you'd like me to go over them before I get the lady's wine."

Dax and Cori exchanged a glance, then Dax said, "Sure. Fire away."

The night's special included grilled trout almandine, seafood pasta, and a thick New York strip. Once he'd covered all the dishes, sides, and prices, the waiter left.

"I understand you just retired from the military," Cori said.

"Army."

"Thank you for your service."

Dax gave a noncommittal nod. He'd heard that a lot and was never sure when and if the person was sincere or was giving a standard response. In this case, he elected to believe her because he wanted to.

"How long were you in?" she asked.

"Went after college and medically retired last year."

"ROTC?"

"Yes, ma'am."

"Oh, good Lord. Don't ma'am me. I'm younger than you are."

He grinned. "Sorry. Force of habit."

"How old are you?"

"Thirty-six. You?"

"Thirty-three."

Before she could ask more, the waiter came back,

set Cori's wine on the table, took their orders, and left.

"And you're a psychiatrist?"

"Psychologist. No drugs. We're all talk. Well, actually, we listen more than talk. But I have a medical adviser if I feel a patient needs more than I can provide. So be warned, I listen all day, so I'll probably talk your ear off."

He grinned. That sounded wonderful to him. She had a soothing voice that calmed him while still stoking his lust. That made no sense, but he would go with it. "Why did you decide you to become a psychologist?" He lifted his iced tea to his suddenly dry mouth.

"Growing up, it seemed like all my friends came to me with their problems. I was good with listening and letting them work out their own problems." She shrugged. "I liked being needed, I guess. What about you? Why the military?"

"With all the bad things in the world, I'd hoped to make a difference. But let's talk about you and Whispering Springs. You grew up here, right?"

Before she answered, the waiter reappeared and set two house salads in front of them. After they both declined fresh ground pepper, he gestured for her to go on talking.

She took a sip of wine. "Born and raised here. My family's roots go back to my grandparents. We're not the oldest family in the area, that'd be the Montgomerys, but we're a close second."

"How did your grandparents end up here?"

"It's Texas; how else? Cattle ranching."

"Your family still in the business?"

She shook her head. "Nope. Dad's in real estate development. Mom works in his office doing real estate sales."

"So, the ranch is gone?"

"No, no. We still live at Rock Creek Ranch. Dad leases the acreage to the Montgomerys for their cattle. We have horses and a couple of goats, but that's it."

"I gather you ride?"

"Heck yeah. Mom had me in the saddle a couple of months after I was born. You?"

He shook his head. "Not really. I've been on a horse, but can't say I ride."

"I'll teach you," she offered up in a hurry.

He shrugged. "I don't know." He thought about his missing left foot and shin. Riding would probably be impossible, and even if it was possible, he didn't want to embarrass himself. He assumed everybody in Texas could ride.

"Sorry, but you have to ride if you live here," she said with a bright grin. "Texas has laws about these things. Oh, and you have to have a pair of boots and a cowboy hat too."

He narrowed his eyes. "I'm pretty sure you're joking, but hell, this is Texas. I suspect your legislature could pass something like that and get it signed."

She laughed. "It wouldn't shock me."

Their waiter reappeared and set two sizzling steaks with all the trimmings on the table.

"Besides riding," Dax said, "what other things did you enjoy doing growing up?"

"Mom put me on the horse. Dad put me at the end of a telescope. We'd spend hours looking at the planets, watching for shooting stars, and finding the various constellations." She sighed. "Dad was super busy with his company when I was growing up, but he always found the time to go out into the fields and set up the telescope with me."

"Nice memories."

"Yeah."

"Why did you stay? In Texas, I mean. There are a lot of other places to go."

She shook her head. "Poor, poor delusional man. This is Texas, the greatest state ever admitted to the union. Why would anyone want to leave?"

He chuckled. "I see."

They talked about football—her a Cowboys fan, him a Patriots fan—rodeos and colleges. Anytime the conversation drifted his way, he would bounce the topic back to her. He knew if they began talking about him, she'd want to know about the scars. He was pretty sure he'd seen her studying them while she thought he wasn't looking. And then the next thing he'd know, she'd be psychoanalyzing him.

No, thank you. He didn't need that...even if it was possible his mother thought he did.

"Dessert?"

Dax startled, his hands clenching into fists around the knife and fork in his hands. He took a deep breath, relaxed the tension in his fingers, and plastered on what he figured was a less-than-friendly smile. Their waiter stood beside their table holding a tray of sample desserts.

"Dessert?" he asked Cori.

She padded her abdomen. "I really shouldn't. I'm pretty sure nothing on that tray is on my diet."

He frowned. "Diet? That's ridiculous. You don't need to be on a diet."

She smiled. "You're sweet, but we both know that's a lie."

What was she talking about? She looked great. Maybe she had some curves, but frankly, he was a little tired of thin, muscular women. Growing up, when his mom had hugged him, he'd loved her soft, cushiony feel. Here was another woman brainwashed into thinking a curve was a bad thing.

"Tell you what; let's split one."

Her face lit up, and he knew he'd produced the right answer.

"Really?"

"Sure, why not? What's your favorite?"

"Hmm." She studied the dessert tray like she was memorizing facts for an exam. "It's been so long," she muttered. Looking at him, she asked, "What do you think about warm chocolate pecan pie with vanilla ice cream?"

"Sounds like heaven on a plate. That's what we'll have," he told the waiter. "Bring two spoons."

"Great choice," the waiter said.

"Chocolate pecan pie is one of my favorites," Dax said. "It's like you read my mind."

"In my line of work, reading minds would be an excellent advantage." She frowned. "On second thought, I'm not sure I would really want to see into some of my patients' minds."

He arched a brow. "Really? We haven't talked about your work at all."

"Next time," she said.

Seriously? Was she suggesting there would be a next time? He smiled.

Dessert was as delicious and decadent as he'd hoped. When the last bite remained, they playfully battled with spoons for it until he surrendered.

After he'd paid for the meal, and they were making their way through the building to the parking lot, she turned and said in a low voice, "Don't think I didn't notice. I did. We should talk about that." Then she turned back around and walked outside, Dax close on her heels.

Fuck. He'd known it. His damn scars. His scars had repulsed her. What woman wouldn't be? Of fucking course, a psychologist would know exactly how to handle him over a simple meal. God, he was such a fool. She hadn't been attracted to him. She'd simply been kind to him, which pissed him off more than if she'd just made up an excuse and left.

At first, he considered letting her leave without confronting her comment, but fuck her and her professional politeness. He'd rather she had lied to him than see him as some pitiful man who needed attention.

Outside, he grasped her upper arm and led her

over to a quiet spot. "What the hell did that snide comment mean?"

Her eyes opened wide.

Ha, he thought. *Caught you*.

Her back stiffened. "What snide comment?"

"The one inside as we were leaving. The one about my facial and neck scars."

Her mouth dropped in a gasp. "What? What are you talking about?"

"These," he replied, jabbing his left cheek with his finger. "And here." He pulled the collar of his shirt aside and punched at the burn scars on his neck and ear. "These are what I'm talking about."

Her eyes narrowed. "Follow me."

She grabbed his hand and started walking. He let her lead him to a four-door, late-model sedan. Once there, she dropped his hand and leaned close to say, "Of course I saw your scars, but so what? Everyone has scars."

"Not everyone has these kinds of scars." He indicated what he was talking about with a wave of his hand. "And there are more you can't see. Did you also notice I'm missing part of a leg?"

Her mouth tightened into a straight line. "No, I didn't know you were missing part of a leg, but so what? You should wear those scars with pride. You survived something horrific. Something that would kill most people, but it didn't kill you. You lived. You fought death and won. You are a survivor."

"Then what were you talking about with your 'don't think I didn't notice' comment?"

She frowned. "The fact we talked about me all night and nothing about you. I wanted to know more about you, about growing up, and life in the military. That's what I meant. You directed the conversation back to me every time, and that was fine for tonight. But you didn't begin to let me know you."

After withdrawing her keys from her purse, she unlocked her car, opened the door, and stepped into the open space. The car's driver's door stood between them like a wall.

Her gaze met his and held. "Maybe your scars are more than what can be seen on the outside. You should think about that." She began to slide into her car and stopped. "Get some help. Talk to a professional, and it can't be me." She smiled. "You're a little old for my clientele and besides, I would never date a client." Pinching his chin between her thumb and forefinger, she pulled him toward her and gave him a soft kiss. "Up until about five minutes ago, it was a wonderful evening. Call me when you understand that scars mean you fought and won."

She slid under the steering wheel and pulled out of the lot without once looking back.

Shit. Was she right? Was he making more of his scars than anyone else? Had he exaggerated the damage?

No, he didn't think so. They were horrific—disfiguring and life-altering. His entire life had certainly been altered after that explosion. His least favorite part of the day was shaving, as he was required to see them reflected back at him from the bathroom mirror. He'd considered growing a beard, but hair didn't grow well through his burn scars. They were too thick.

Glancing into his rearview mirror, he looked at his face and neck. No, those fucking scars were as bad as he thought. Dr. Cori Lambert, a professional psychologist, simply knew what to say to minimize damage to his feelings.

Depression's strong undertow pulled wanted to drown him. Even the memory of the delicious kiss Cori had left on his lips couldn't stem the tide. He struggled to breathe against the pressure weighing down his chest. Each breath took enormous energy as though sucking in all his air through a thin straw. By the time he got back to Marc's house, he was exhausted.

For once, fate smiled on him. The house was empty—no prying questions from his sister or brother about the date.

Sleep that night, like every night since he'd left the hospital didn't come easily. Finding a comfortable position in bed was akin to finding a needle in a haystack...possible, but only after hours of work. And in those brief moments when he did sleep, his dreams were filled with the explosion that had almost killed him and had killed three of his team.

The thick smoke.

The eardrum bursting noise.

The hysterical screams of his men and the civilians in their caravan.

Every goddamn night.

When his clock rolled over to three a.m., he gave up on sleep. He sat up and swung his legs to the floor. Sitting on the side of his bed, his head in his hands, his face throbbed in all the scarred spots. With each thump of his heart, the scars screamed, *Here we are. Here we are.*

He picked up the book on his bedside table—a mystery/suspense by a popular author. After three pages, he realized he had no idea what had happened. His brain was still locked in his dream.

Downstairs, he flicked on the television as a distraction. However, the channels were mostly running infomercials and news. Frankly, he'd had all the news he could stand for a while, so he watched infomercial after infomercial.

One of the infomercials was for a tile steam cleaner. When he caught himself seriously considering buying one, he shut off the TV. He didn't even have a house. What would he need with a steam cleaner?

He set the coffeemaker to brew and headed for the shower. A hot water spray usually loosened the knotted muscles in his neck and back. The downside, however, was that the warmer water, the redder and more conspicuous his scars would become. Looser muscles or flaming scars? His daily decision dilemma. Shower water temperature decisions always rested on whether he had to be seen or not seen. Since it was still early in the day, and he had nowhere to go, hot water and unknotted muscles won.

After toweling off, he looked in the mirror to see if he could skip shaving for another day. Internally, he snarled at his scarred flesh. He couldn't even grow a beard to camouflage the damage. Hair struggled to push through the thick, scarred flesh, and if it did, the resulting beard was skimpy and patchy. Shaving the area was a pain in the ass, but fate hadn't left him many choices.

As he gently shaved his hideous face, he wondered, as he often did, if it wouldn't have been better if he'd died that day. Why did he deserve to live when others on his team hadn't made it? Jones, one of his guys, had a wife and two kids when he'd been killed. Woods had died with his wedding only a couple of months away. And Stephens, the poor bastard, had survived their nightmare vacation to the land of the Taliban only to discovered a fatal tumor growing in his brain.

And yet here he was, a man with no wife, no children, no one relying on him, and he'd lived to see another day. Why? He wasn't sure he believed in God or Buddha or some higher power who had infinite knowledge. If something like that existed, surely it or he or she, or whatever it was, wouldn't have let him live, instead of taking a good man like Jones.

But then he'd picture his mother's face when he'd awakened in his hospital room in Germany. He remembered the feel of his father's arms so tight about his shoulders that he thought his bones would break. Recalled the buckets of tears both of them had shed when they'd thought him unconscious. He'd had to keep going, for them, if nothing else.

After dressing in jeans and a long-sleeve Henley, he headed down for coffee.

"Morning," Dax said to his brother. "You're up early."

Marc shrugged. "Didn't sleep very well. Thanks for making the coffee, by the way."

"Am I bothering you with all my restlessness? I can leave."

"No. Don't be stupid. If I wanted you gone, I wouldn't hint. I'd pack up your shit and set it on the front porch, so let's stop having this conversation."

Dax scoffed at Marc's comment and took a seat at the table, a cup of hot coffee cradled between his hands.

Being only two years apart in age, Dax and Marc had grown up as tight as two brothers could be. Sure, they'd had their fisticuffs and arguments over the years, but he knew beyond a shadow of a doubt that his brother would be there for him regardless of the situation.

Dax was also sure that Marc was being honest about kicking him out if he didn't want him there. He appreciated that his brother treated him much as he always had, even though Marc had commented a few times that Dax had scared the crap out of him with his almost-dying stunt.

Their mom, however, still had trouble with Dax's injuries and tended to hover. That was the primary reason Dax was sure he wouldn't settle in Maine. Their beloved mother would drive him crazy.

"How was the date?" Marc asked.

Dax winced. "It was going okay, but we kind of ended on a bad note."

"What did you do?"

Dax feigned outrage. "What makes you think I did something?"

Marc lifted his coffee mug in a salute. "Because I know you. What did you do?"

"Maybe, I might have—and I do mean *might have*—misinterpreted something Cori said."

"Ah. Want to tell me what she said?"

"No." Dax didn't like to even think of how poorly he'd handled the situation. The scene in the parking lot had played over and over in his head since he'd gotten up. Had Cori been right? Was he more focused on his scars than the people he met?

"Okay. Before you screwed up things, how did it go?"

"Okay." He took a long slug of coffee.

"Just okay?"

"Well, maybe a little better than okay, or it had been until I blew it. Cori Lambert is very much like you described her. Smart. Funny. Very attractive. I liked her. Oh, and here's the weird thing. She and I ran into each other at Nelson's yesterday afternoon. Literally, run into each other. She crashed her cart into mine. Odd, huh?"

"Not really. Whispering Springs is a small town. If you need groceries, your only choices are Nelson's and a couple of other smaller markets. You can count on running into people you know every time you go in. You going to ask her out again?"

"I don't know. Probably not."

"I don't get you. You liked her. She must not have found your personality too offensive since she stayed through the whole meal. Why not give it a second chance? Or did you screw up that badly? Want to confide about the horrible thing you did?"

Dax shook his head. "No, not really." He stood to get a second cup of coffee. "I'll think about calling her. But I'm telling you, if I do, I might be eating a ton of crow."

"Add barbeque sauce. It helps anything."

Dax laughed. "Want me to make pancakes as payment for all that sage advice you gave?"

"I've got a better idea. Let's go down to the Sunshine Café and get us the best gut-busting, carb-loaded, calorie-laden breakfast in Whispering Springs."

"God. How can I turn that down? Want me to wake up Sami and see if she wants to go?"

"She's gone for the day."

Dax's eyebrows rose. "Already?"

"Not gone for good. She and I had a long talk last night and she understands why I can't hire her. I called in a couple of favors and got her interviews with the Whispering Springs Chief of Police, Shade Gruber, and another with Sheriff Kyle Monroe one county over. She's got great creds from the military, so one of them will probably have a position for her.

Monroe could only see her at seven this morning, so she's headed over there now,"

"Don't tell her that you had to call in favors for these interviews."

"Of course, I won't tell her. I'm not crazy. Oh, did I mention you're paying for breakfast?"

Dax shook his head. "Why am I not surprised by that news?"

Becky's Sunshine Café was everything Dax expected and more. When they walked in at six-thirty, the place was already jumping. Most of the bright yellow and white booths were occupied, as were most of the tables. For a moment, Dax considered leaving on his sunglasses to dim all the bright yellow.

"Hey, Sheriff," a female voice called through the opening to the kitchen. "Grab a booth and I'll send Margie right over."

"Morning, Elle," Marc said with a wave. "Thanks."

He led Dax to a booth at the back of the café, and the two men slid in opposite each other.

"That's Becky," Marc said. "She owns this place. Nicest woman in the world unless you bring up her ex-husband." He shook his head with a laugh. "She can produce some of the most creative cussing I've ever heard."

"Which is saying something given your MP background."

"Exactly." Marc looked toward the door and waved. Dax slid around on the bench to see who'd come into the diner.

"Who is it?"

"Jason and Cash Montgomery."

"You really do run into everyone, huh?"

Two tall, physically fit men walked up to the booth. Both men were clad in what Dax had decided was the required Texas garb of jeans, flannel shirt, boots, and cowboy hat.

"Morning," one of the men said.

"Morning, Jason. Cash," Marc said.

"This must be your brother," Jason said, extending his hand. "Jason Montgomery." He lifted his chin toward the other man. "My brother Cash."

Dax shook both men's hands. "Dax Cooper."

"Worst secret in Whispering Springs," Cash said. "If you don't know it, gossip spreads here like soft butter on hot toast. Trust me. I even know you had a date with Cori Lambert last night."

Dax's head jerked back in surprise. "You're kidding."

Cash laughed. "Paige and I were having dinner at Rick's last night. I saw you walk through with Cori. The town's small but not that small. It should've taken about forty-eight hours to get that news on the gossip vine."

"Good Lord," Dax said with a roll of his eyes.

"You want to join us?" Marc asked. "We just ordered."

"Thanks, but no," Jason said. "We're meeting Travis and Mitch for our monthly *surviving marriage* breakfast."

Marc nodded. "Got it." He lifted a hand and shot

a finger toward the door. "Travis and Mitch are just walking in. Good to see you both."

"Good to meet you," Dax said.

Jason and Cash started toward the table where the other men had taken seats.

Jason snapped his fingers and walked back.

"Marc, I talked to the Hanson family yesterday. They said they'll give you a week, ten days tops, but then the property will have to go on the market. Have you made a decision?"

"Not yet. It's a lot of money."

"But a hell of a deal."

"I know, I know," Marc said with a long sigh. "I'll let you know something by the middle of next week."

"Great. Talk to you then."

After Jason walked away, Dax asked, "You're looking at buying some property?"

"Looking at it, thinking about it, but I just don't know. It would be one hell of an undertaking on my own, running a ranch and being the full-time-sheriff. I might be biting off more than I can chew."

"I'd love to see what you're looking at."

"Okay. We can run out this morning, unless you have something else you have to do."

Dax shrugged. "Nothing on my plate, but laundry, and that can wait."

Conversation at their table slowed considerably as both men dug into their gut-busting breakfasts. However, as soon as the last sip of coffee was swallowed, Marc said, "Ready? We can head out to the Hanson place now." He slid from the booth.

Dax looked at his empty cup. He'd really love another jolt of caffeine, but with Marc standing there looking like a kid on Christmas morning ready to display what Santa had bought, Dax nodded and stood. "Ready when you are."

The drive took Dax to an area of the county he hadn't driven through yet, but he might as well have. The gently rolling hills with green pastures dotted with cattle looked much like his self-guided tour from a couple of days ago.

Marc pointed toward the right side of the truck. "That's the Lambert's place."

Dax saw a sign that read Cloverdale Ranch. "Cloverdale?"

"Yup. Her parents' names are Clover and Dale Lambert." Marc chuckled. "They're quite a pair."

"Hmm. Looks like a big place."

"It's about fifteen hundred acres or so of prime grazing land. They inherited it when Clover's parents died. Guess that was about twenty years ago, but they were already living on the ranch with her parents at the time." Marc glanced over. "Impressed?"

"Hell, yeah. Is the place you're considering comparable to this?"

Marc laughed. "Not hardly. About one-fifth the size, but it does have a nice creek that runs through it and a few ponds."

Dax's head turned to continue studying

Cloverdale Ranch as Marc drove past. "What you're showing me is that Cori comes from money...?"

"Oh, yeah. Tons of it."

That wasn't good. What did he have to give a woman who could buy anything she wanted? He had nothing to offer. No job. Damaged legs. And apparently, according to Cori, a screwed-up mind.

"She kissed me."

Marc slowed the truck and looked at Dax. "Cori?"

Dax nodded.

"Before or after you put your size fourteens into your mouth?"

Dax snorted. "After."

"Well, that's something positive, right? At least she didn't slap you."

Dax laughed. "I can always count on you to be supportive."

"No, I'm being serious. If you like Cori and want to see her again, I think the door is open, you know?"

"I don't know." He shrugged. "Could've been a kiss-off too."

"Only one way to know. Call her and ask her out again, I mean, if you want to."

Dax shrugged. He wouldn't mind seeing Cori again, but she was so out of his league. Smarter, richer, and certainly more attractive and sexier.

His thoughts were interrupted when the click, click, click of Marc's turn signal penetrated his brain. His brother turned onto a washed-out gravel lane and stopped at the metal pole gate across it. Marc hopped out, unlocked the padlock on the chain holding the gate shut, climbed back in, and drove through.

"You have the key?" Dax asked.

He nodded. "I've had it for a couple of years. Sam and Ruth Hanson lived here alone for the last ten years or so. Raised five children, all of whom married and moved out of state. They'd hoped that one of their kids would come home and take over the farm, but not one of them had any interest. For the past couple of years, I've been coming by and checking on Sam and Ruth and letting their kids know if they were doing okay.

"Came by about six months ago, and both of them had died sometime between my visits. M.E. said natural deaths due to old age."

"How old were they?" Dax asked as they bumped along the drive.

"Early nineties. Their deaths were no surprise and definitely not suspicious in any way. All their children, spouses and their children came to town and gave them a real nice funeral. The whole town turned out." He glanced over at Dax. "That's the way Whispering Springs is. Everybody came and paid their respects. Anyway, the Hanson offspring took everything they wanted from the house and property, but none of them wanted the ranch. They knew I'd fallen in love with the place, so, they offered me first right of refusal. If I want it, they'll give me a good deal. Otherwise, it'll go on the open market."

"I have no idea what property prices are around here. What's a good deal?"

"This place has a little over five-hundred acres. On the open market, they'd be asking about two million or two-and-a-half million, maybe more. A selling price under that would be a good deal."

Dax whistled. "You've got to be kidding."

"You have to remember that we're only a little over an hour from Dallas and yet, we still have that small-town feel. People eat that stuff up. And we're close to the Fort Worth stockyards, which is valuable since so many ranchers raise cattle. Those four spring-fed ponds add a lot to the value."

Dax looked around at the tall green grass blowing in the spring breeze. "What'd they grow here?"

"Nothing in the last ten years. Used to be a small cattle operation." Marc pointed out his window. "If you look over there, you'll see the cattle pens and chutes still standing. Probably in horrible repair, much like the road getting in here. Some of the outbuildings are still standing, as is the house and barn. But the house...Well, just wait."

Shaking his head, Dax said, "Two mill. You don't have that kind of money. Hell, nobody in our family has that kind of money."

"I know," Marc said in a dejected voice.

"What about a loan?"

"Let's take a look around," he replied instead of answering Dax's question.

The clapboard house had been standing a long time in its spot. What had once been white paint now flecked off the exterior with a brush of a hand. Not only would the house need a serious scrubbing and painting, but some sections would have to be replaced.

"As you can see," Marc said, "the house needs some work. It's been empty since the Hansons died."

Dax brushed the paint flecks off his hands. "Anyone with vision can see that, Bro."

He followed Marc up a couple of concrete block steps to the porch. The flooring groaned as the two large men crossed to the front door. Dragging another key from his pocket, Marc unlocked and swung open an old-fashioned window-paneled door. The action stirred the layer of dust inside.

Dax coughed as he followed Marc inside. "Two million, you say."

Marc chuckled. "Trust me. You aren't buying this property for the main house. It's the land it's sitting on that holds all the value."

"The house is larger than it looks from the outside," Dax said.

Marc nodded. "Yeah. Looks like they added on as children came. Still, it's only a four-bedroom, two-bathroom house."

"Has potential," Dax murmured.

"I know," Marc said excitedly. "That's what I thought." He released a breath. "I'm so glad you think so too."

Dax winced. The house probably did have some worth, but holy hell, it was going to be a ton of work, not to mention money, to get it livable in this century.

"Come on. Let me show you the barn."

Dax followed his brother out a back door to a large, old-fashioned barn in amazingly good shape. As soon as the doors swung open, dust and dirt flew in the air, making both men sneeze.

"Guess this needs a good cleaning," Marc said.

Dax nodded. "Why don't you go on and lock up the house? I think I'm going to wander around a bit."

Marc headed back to the house while Dax took a closer look at the barn. It seemed sturdy. No leaning. No wood rot that he could find. A couple of field mice scurried across the floor inside one of the stalls, but he assumed mice in a barn was to be expected, but then, what did he know about barns? Give him a rifle, and he could strip and reassemble it blindfolded. He was out of his depth with ranches and cattle. He was still preparing how to tell Marc that this place needed a ton of work when Marc stuck his head through the barn door.

"We gotta roll. Accident about a mile from here."

Dax breathed a sigh of relief. He was off the hot seat for now.

Four

Cori kicked off her heels and fell face-first on her bed. Sunday lunch with her parents was usually a trial, but today? Geez. The Spanish Inquisition had nothing on her mother's grilling about her date with Dax Cooper. No burning at the stake, but she'd definitely felt the heat.

She knew her mom loved her and wanted her to be happy, but good grief. It was one date, and one that had ended on a less than positive note. In fact, she would be surprised if she heard from him again.

A weight pounced onto her back with a thump. Four tiny paws walked around in a circle before setting into the small of her back with a purr.

"Beatrice, get off. You're smashing my full gut."

The twelve-pound lilac Siamese cat flexed her nails into Cori's back and purred louder. With a laugh, Cori reached around her waist and pushed her fur baby off. "I'm thinking you need to go on a diet."

Beatrice glared at Cori with her blue eyes before flipping her tail into the air and jumping off the bed.

Cori grinned. "Sorry, girl. You're perfect. I swear."

As though considering and then rejecting the compliment, the cat paused and then strode from the bedroom without a backward glance.

"And that's why I should have saved a dog at the pound," she called after her thankless pet that she loved more than anything.

With a sigh, she stood and changed into more comfortable clothing for an afternoon of updating clients' records, something with an elastic waistband that would allow her to breathe. She barefooted it to the dining room where the stack of folders awaited. She glanced outside to the perfect spring day and then back to the manila folders, back to the sun, back to the table, then sighed and sat down. Man, she hated when her responsible side overruled her impulsive side.

Three hours later, she closed the last file—not that she'd been working the entire time. There was that short nap about an hour in. Still, she was finished for now.

She leaned back in her chair with an exhausted sigh. She always chided her patients about being honest with themselves. Lately, she'd been thinking she should take her own advice. She worked all week, and still had to do recordkeeping on her weekends. She was tired and burned out. She'd been questioning continuing on her chosen career path. The thought of sitting behind a desk day in and day out for the rest of her working life made her eyes twitch. Her entire youth had been spent outdoors, sometimes climbing trees, or designing floral leis and once building a fort, but a lot of her time had been on the back of her beloved gelding, Elvis. She still missed that cantankerous bastard.

She'd just poured herself a wine when her cellphone chimed an alert for a text.

Dax: *I know it's late notice but do you want to go look at some stars tonight? Oh, this is Dax.*

Before she could reply, her phone buzzed again.

Dax: *I'm providing dinner. Did I mention that?*

A smile began to pull at the corners of her lips. She could give him another chance, although she felt sure he had some issues he needed to work through. But he wasn't a patient, so no wearing her head-shrinker hat tonight. Besides, he was pretty cute.

Cori: *Well, it is late but lucky for you, I have no plans. Stars, you say? Have a particular place in mind?*

Dax: *Yes, but let's make it a surprise. Pick you up about 7:30. That too late?*

Cori: *Not if we are looking at stars. It won't be dark until nine anyway, so sure. That time works for me. See you then*

She had some time to get ready. Now, what does one wear to go stargazing? She settled on jeans, boots, a red tank top and a red and black plaid overshirt. She was rolling up the long sleeves when her doorbell chimed. A kaleidoscope of butterflies exploded in her gut. Pressing her hand to her abdomen did nothing to quell the tugs.

"Coming," she called, hurrying to the front door.

Her breath caught when she came face to face with Dax again. The early evening light glistened in his hair, and when he smiled, those dimples popped onto his cheeks. Her knees wobbled.

How could he begin to think that any facial scar could detract from the handsome curves and angles? She remembered one guy from high school whose acne scars had been way worse. Dax's scars, which were barely visible, made him look dangerous and intriguing, as though he had secrets only he knew. Her very own James Bond.

"Hi," he said. "Glad you could make it. Ready?"

"I am." She grabbed a sweater off a hook by the door.

"Not sure you're going to need that sweater."

Tossing it over her arm, she said, "It's Texas. You never know. Temps have been a little cooler than normal." She shrugged. "Better to have it and not need it than need it and not have it."

Her libido reminded her that getting cold could also lead to snuggling. Her libido called her an idiot.

It'd been a long time since she'd been on a date quite like this one. Maybe as far back as high school. Usually, her dates now meant indoor dining, maybe a show or concert, and then home. But back in high school, she and her friends would build big bonfires and sit around them for hours.

With her love of the outdoors, he couldn't have suggested anything better than an outside activity.

Grabbing the passenger side hold bar, she pulled herself up into the truck. When she was settled, Dax closed the door behind her. The truck was old but spotless. She sniffed, and the scent of wax and cherry filled her senses. He'd cleaned the truck...for her. Her troop of tiny butterflies tumbled around, and she smiled. If he'd wanted to impress her, mission accomplished.

Dax slid behind the wheel and looked at her. "You might recognize the road we'll be headed down."

"Really?" She arched her eyebrows. "Now, you've got me curious."

Her curiosity didn't last long. The minute he turned onto her parents' road, she turned toward him.

"My parents live on this road."

"I know."

"Are we going to their house?"

His only answer was an arched eyebrow and a smile.

There was a lustful tug just behind her navel. The tug sunk lower in her pelvis.

He drove past the turnoff for her childhood home and continued driving.

She playfully elbowed his muscular arm, which was akin to jabbing a warm log. "Now, you've got me really curious about where we're going."

When he slowed to turn, she nodded. "The Hanson place. I didn't know they'd sold it."

"They haven't, or at least they haven't yet."

He pulled to a stop, climbed from the truck to unlock the gate, and returned. After he was inside the fenced acreage, he shut the gate.

"I'm assuming you have permission to be here?"

He held up the keys. "From the country sheriff himself."

She laughed. "Well, if we get arrested for trespassing, at least I know who to call."

The truck bumped and bucked down the unpaved drive until he took the turn leading to the barn. Driving past the faded, weathered building, he took them into a field. From the crushed grass, she could tell this was not the first time someone had driven this way.

He followed the trail through the high grass until he pulled to a stop near a pond she was intimately familiar with.

"The Hanson swimming hole," she said and clapped her hands together. "I haven't been here in ages." She looked at him. "I didn't bring a swim suit and besides, isn't it a tad cool for skinny dipping?"

He chuckled. "Not to mention that cold water causes shrinkage."

She was laughing when he opened her door. "Very funny."

His response was a grin that stirred the embers of lust. Maybe he'd always had the slightly crooked grin, or it could have been the effect of the scar on his cheek, but either way, the result made her heart sing. He possessed a deadly weapon in that smile, and she suspected he had no idea.

He helped her from the truck and she followed him to the back. There, he dropped the tailgate and pulled a couple of recliners from the back along with a cooler and a basket.

"Dinner," she said. "I'm starving. What do we have?"

He set up the chairs and put the cooler between them. "Fried chicken, potato salad, rolls, and brownies."

Her mouth watered. "Sounds yummy."

They settled into the chairs, both of them holding plates laden with food.

"Now, if you tell me that you made all this, I may swoon," she said and pulled off a piece of breast meat with her teeth.

"No, ma'am. I make a mean omelet, but that's about it."

"I love a mean omelet. I'll look forward to it." She tried to make her voice light with a tease, but to her ears, it sounded like a request for another date. Was it? She wasn't sure, but maybe.

He nodded. "Great." He pretended to write on a piece of paper while muttering, "Learn to make a mean omelet."

She laughed.

They sat, not talking as they ate. Around them, night fell. The smell of fresh spring grass competed with the aroma of fried chicken. Male tree frogs began their nightly calls for female companionship.

~

Cori swallowed a pinch of biscuit and leaned back in the chair with a sigh. "This is so good. I love being out here." Turning her face toward him, she said, "After I got your text, I looked up what was happening tonight." She reached out and touched his arm. Thick, ropey muscles tensed under her fingers. She hoped the physical reaction was due to him liking her touch and not an adverse reaction to being touched. "I love a good meteor shower. I'm so glad I'm not going to miss it. Thank you."

She gave his hard bicep a squeeze and removed her hand.

"I know you're a psychologist, but I'm not sure exactly what you do."

Talking required that she swallow the hunk of chicken she'd torn off. She held up one finger as in, "Give me a minute," chewed and swallowed.

"I work with at-risk kids," she said.

"And that means?"

"Foster kids who are not adjusting, teens struggling with personal issues, maybe failing grades or family issues, you know? Things like that."

"How do they end up with you? Wait. That didn't come out right. What I mean is I am sure they don't refer themselves to you. Teens aren't that self-aware."

She chuckled. "Don't I know it. They're sent to me by school counselors, juvenile courts, teachers, and sometimes, parents. But you're right in that they don't show up at my door without a requirement to do so."

"Sounds like a tough job."

"It is." She sighed. "I've been thinking of doing something else. I love working with my patients, but being stuck in an office all day sucks." She shifted until she could set her empty plate on the ground and then turned toward him. "I was raised outside. When I wasn't in school, I was on a horse, or mucking the barn, or working in mom's garden. In the summer, I stayed as tan as your boots. So did my sisters. But we've been over my life. What about you? Were you an indoor kid or an outdoor kid?"

This was the first time she'd directly asked him about his upbringing. She was tired of talking about herself. She wanted to know more about Dax Cooper, and after she'd been up-front with him about his evasiveness at the end of their date on Friday, she wasn't going to accept a redirect tonight.

"I was a typical boy, I guess. Rode bikes, broke my arm wrestling with my brother, tortured my little sister with frogs and spiders, and had to be forced to do my summer reading."

"Forced to read," she said in a shocked voice. "How horrible. I'm surprised your parents weren't reported to the authorities."

He laughed. "I was an adult and overseas when I discovered that I actually enjoyed reading. But back when I was fourteen or so, I was much more interested in chasing girls."

"And catching them," she added.

"And catching them," he agreed.

"Why the military?"

He shrugged. "I didn't have a clue what I wanted to do after high school. My mom's a college professor, but you probably knew that since our mothers are Facebook friends or whatever it's called."

"I didn't know that," she said. "Actually, I didn't know my mom was on that. What about your dad?"

"He owned a shipyard until a few years ago. Built custom boats for folks with too much money."

She laughed. "If only I had that problem."

He smiled, and she felt an electrical zap run through her veins.

"Hold on," she said as she stood. Grabbing her lounge chair, she turned one-hundred-and-eighty degrees, walked around to his other side, and replaced the chair so her head and shoulders were aligned with his again, only this time her legs pointed south and his pointed north.

"There," she said. "Much better. I was getting a crick in my neck."

"Clever lady."

"Thanks. Now, we were talking about you and growing up. You were saying your dad builds boats?"

"He did, but he sold the business a couple of years ago. Mom teaches at the University of Maine in the Math department."

"You said you have a brother and a sister. Where are they?"

"My brother lives in Whispering Springs. My sister just left the military, and I guess she's trying to decision where to settle."

"Whispering Springs, huh? Do I know him?"

Dax shrugged. "Maybe. Marc Singer?"

She laughed. "And that's how you got permission from the county sheriff to be here. You and Marc have different last names."

He took a long swallow of iced tea and then nodded. "Mom's first husband, Marc's father, died while she was pregnant with Marc. A snowmobile accident. She met and married my and Sami's father when Marc was six months old."

"Sami is?"

"My sister, Samantha."

"Why didn't your dad adopt him and make him a Cooper too?"

"He did, but Marc went back to the Singer name after he and Dad had a falling out—and before you ask, I don't know what they argued over."

"Hmm, how did your dad feel about that?"

"Now, that sounds like something a psychologist would ask."

She smiled. "Force of habit."

"You know men don't talk about feelings," he said with a chuckle. "Enough about me. Let's talk about you."

"One more question."

"Fine," he said with a sigh. "What?"

She sensed the invisible walls going up around him. She'd seen it a million times with her patients. All of them so afraid she was going to ask a question that would break them, or hurt them somehow. If only she could make them understand that sometimes talking about the big, scary subject could tame it, or at least lessen the hold the monster had on their lives.

In Dax's case, she suspected the big, scary monster was the event that gave him his scars and changed how he saw himself. But she wasn't his therapist. She was his date. She didn't have to know everything about his past self and past events to know that she liked his present self...very much.

Resting her hand on his shoulder, she leaned forward and asked, "Would you mind if I kissed you, or is that too forward?"

Five

Dax's heart rate kicked up a few notches—well, maybe more than a few. He glanced over at the beautiful woman sitting on his unaffected side. Sure, he looked good from this side, but...

"Sorry," Cori said, her voice strained. "I shouldn't have..."

Dax caught her hand as she began to withdraw it. "I think I would like that."

They moved toward each other at the same time, their lips meeting in the space between the arms on the chairs. Her lips were, as he remembered from their previous date, soft and full and plush. His stomach clenched as his lust—long dormant—awoke at her touch. If this was a dream, he didn't want to wake up for a long time.

He pulled back and fell deeply into her rich brown eyes.

"Whew," she said. "Glad to get that over with."

He startled and frowned. "Excuse me?"

She laughed and touched his unaffected cheek. "I mean, I'm always nervous about that first kiss on a date." With a shrug, she added, "I wanted to get it out of the way to still my nerves."

"You're nervous?" His heart sank. Was she nervous because she was attracted to him, or nervous because she wasn't attracted but thought a kiss would make him feel better? "Why?"

"Well, yeah." She swept her hand in his direction. "You're a sexy war hero who..." she sniffed, "smells like an exotic vacation. I don't know what your cologne is, but I love it."

Pleasure rippled through him. He was glad the sun was almost gone. She probably couldn't see his embarrassed flush at her comments. It'd been a very long time since he'd been with a woman. He'd been too busy when he'd been on active duty, and then the last couple of years of surgeries and rehab had taken their toll on his love life, or lack of one.

"Thanks," he muttered. He couldn't answer her cologne question because he had no idea what the brand was. He'd found it in Marc's bathroom, thought it smelled nice, and used it. Buying his own cologne hadn't been high on his to-do list in forever. "Let's clean up and do some stargazing," he said as a way to redirect the conversation.

She smiled. "That's what we're here for."

By the time they'd cleaned up any leftover food and loaded the small table and chairs into the truck bed, night had fallen.

"Do you need help climbing into the back?" Dax asked, gesturing toward the truck bed.

Cori chuckled. "This is Texas, darling. Climbing into the back of trucks is taught right after walking."

Shaking his head with a grin at her reply, he pulled a long box from the backseat. He began assembling the telescope he'd borrowed for the evening.

Cori studied the high-powered scope. "That's a pretty fancy telescope. You didn't tell me you were into stargazing."

He laughed. "I'm not. I borrowed this from my brother. He used to use it for different things, probably surveillance of criminal activities, but he'll never admit it."

"Makes sense. Now, let's get to some stargazing."

"I hope you know how to use this thing," Dax said. "I confess, I don't."

She smiled and patted his cheek. "Don't worry. I'm fluent in telescopes."

"Whew. So, a meteor shower is our show tonight?"

"Yes. But that'll show up when it shows up. Until then, you want to look at stars and constellations?"

"Great. I know nothing about stars, except I could probably find the Big Dipper."

She laughed. "I think all kids are taught to find that."

"And the Little Dipper," he said proudly.

She again stroked his cheek. "Yep, that too." For the next half-hour, she showed him various star constellations. Orion. Canis Major and Minor. Ursa major and minor and Cassiopeia.

Sometimes, he could tell what she was trying to show him, and sometimes not. But through the telescope lens, he could see Saturn, which was a first.

Her knowledge of the stars and the constellations was vast. His brother had been right...she was smarter than him. Too smart? Would she become bored with him quickly? Since the first night he'd met her, he'd wondered why she was single. A beautiful face and a luscious body were usually enough to attract male attention. Toss in her caring, yet funny, personality, and the combination should have made her irresistible. Could it be possible that the men in this town were daunted by her intelligence? He couldn't say he was intimidated, but he was certainly impressed.

"What time is it?" she asked. "I left my phone inside the truck."

Dax pulled out his phone. "Almost ten-fifteen. The report I read said the meteor showers would start about—"

Before he could finish his statement, a streak of fire lit up the skies above them.

"Oh..." Cori said. "It's starting."

That single streak was followed by tens of dozens of white flashes in the dark sky as meteors hurled toward the earth.

Their chairs were sitting side by side in the back of his truck.

Cori reached over, laced her fingers through his,

and squeezed. "Thank you. This is so great. I'm so glad we did this."

"Me, too," he said with a smile that he felt to his toes. It'd been a long time since he'd experienced this kind of peace and acceptance.

Her fingers were slender and soft. In the night breeze, her perfume swirled around his head, intoxicating him with her scent. This first blast of outer space rocks lasted only a short time. If the meteor shower lasted for the next four hours, that'd be fine with him, but he doubted she'd want to sit in this field past midnight.

Dax knew he needed to keep this night on track. He'd asked her out to apologize for how he'd left things after dinner on Friday, and he'd yet to find the nerve to broach the subject.

As the fiery show slowed, he took a deep breath of courage and turned in his chair toward her.

Cori was leaning back in her chair with a happy smile on her face. "That was amazing. I loved it."

"I did too. Listen, I need to tell you something."

Her face wrinkled into a frown. "Okay, what is it?"

"I need to apologize for Friday night."

"For what?"

"For being so sensitive about your comment."

"Your minimal scarring? You think I would be so cruel as to condemn someone based on his looks?"

"Now that I've been around you more, no, I don't, not really. I just...people stare at me, and I know it's the scars."

She shook her head. "Dax, people don't look at your scars."

"Yeah, well, you haven't been in my place. You don't know what it's like."

"I'm people, Dax. I know what I see when I look at you. You're a handsome, extremely attractive man with a pretty mouth, and dimples in his cheeks. And sure, you've got a couple of places on your neck and your face where I can see where you were burned, but so what?"

"You haven't seen my chest," Dax said, disgust in his voice,

She arched a brow. "Gives me something to look forward to." She grinned. "I bet I'll really enjoy that... maybe more than tonight's show."

He shook his head. "Cori, you are one interesting woman."

She laughed. "No, not really. Every woman would feel the same way. We don't look so much at the exterior—"

He interrupted her and said, "Yeah, women do look at the exterior."

She shrugged. "Maybe some do, but you have to remember that because of my job and education, I've long since learned to look past the exterior. There are very handsome men out there who have the darkest, ugliest souls you've ever seen. And then there are some men who aren't as attractive on the outside, but their souls are bright lights of beauty. They are loving and kind and considerate. These men have so much to give to another person. Which one do you think I'd want in my life?"

"Which category am I?" Dax asked.

She chuckled. "We just met, but my money is on you having that bright, loving soul, but your trauma has done as much damage to your inside as your outside. Now, I'm not your therapist, and I never will be, but you need to work with someone to accept the past and move on with your life."

He leaned back in his chair with a sigh and looked up into the night sky. "I can't. I just can't. You don't know."

"You're right. I don't know what happened and I'm not asking what happened."

"I'm not talking so much about me, but I lost men who didn't deserve to die over there. Great men. Loyal men, Men who had promising futures with families and fiancées. Men who were dads to their children and were excited about getting home to see them." He wiped his hand down his face. "It wasn't fair that they died."

"You're right. It wasn't fair. War isn't fair. War takes valuable men and women away from our society and their families. If I had a magic wand or I was the queen of the world..." She snapped her fingers. "We wouldn't have any more wars."

He looked at her. "Hmm, maybe you should be the queen of the world."

She chuckled.

"It's getting late and I know tomorrow is a work day for you."

"It is, and I should be getting home, but Dax, this was extra special for me. You remembered what I said about stargazing with my dad and took me on an adventure that brought me so much happiness. Thank you so much."

He smiled. "It was my pleasure. Maybe we could get dinner this weekend?"

She nodded. "I think I would like that."

When he got her back to her house, he kissed her. This time, he didn't wait for her to initiate the kiss. It was time for him to step up to the plate and show her that he liked her, for so many reasons. Like the previous two kisses, this kiss set his heart racing. This woman was special. How could his mother, all the way up in Maine, know that this daughter of an internet friend would be so extraordinary?

He let himself into Marc's front door and found his brother sitting on the sofa watching the late news.

"Hey. You're still up," Dax said. "Waiting up for me like Dad used to?"

"Yep." He chuckled. "How was the date?"

"It was nice. Thank you for the telescope."

"Sure, no problem. I haven't used it in forever. Did it work okay?"

"Yeah, yeah. It did great."

"How was the meteor shower?"

"Pretty damn cool. You ever see one?"

"Sure, I have. This is Whispering Springs. We don't have much light pollution, so you'll be able to see a lot of things at night."

Dax looked toward the stairs. "Sami already in bed?"

"Nope, she's in Tyler. Apparently, she has a friend from the military who lives there and has gone to stay with her for a couple of days and think about what she wants to do."

"How'd the interviews go?"

"Apparently, good. She got offers from both Chief Gruber and Sheriff Monroe. She has to make a decision about where she wants to live. Here in Whispering Springs or over in Diamond Lakes."

"Whichever one she takes, she'll have to go through a police academy, right?"

"Right. Her biggest obstacle will be learning all the Texas laws she'll have to enforce. The physical side shouldn't be an issue for her. She's in great shape."

"Which offer do you think she'll take?"

"I have no idea. This is our sister we're talking about. Unpredictability is her middle name."

Dax laughed. "Isn't that the truth?"

"But to be honest, I hope she takes the position in Diamond Lakes under Sheriff Monroe."

"Why?"

"It's the nepotism thing."

"Again, why? She won't be in your department."

"I know, I know, but my office works closely with the police department. Our paths would cross. I don't want to put her in a situation where people think she got her job because of her big brother, you know? Or that she's getting some type of favored treatment because of me."

"I get it. Is Gruber the kind of guy who would hire her just because of you?"

Marc laughed. "God, no. He's as hard-nosed as they come. He came out of the Chicago police department as a detective. Worked for the Texas State police before taking the job here. No, he doesn't take much shit from anybody."

"I don't think you have anything to worry about then. If she goes to work with Gruber, she'll be here. If she takes Sheriff Monroe's offer, she won't be too far away. I'm not sure one is better than the other."

"Yeah, well, once again, you, me, and Sami all in one location in the country, and you think Mom isn't going to show up down here? She could throw a monkey wrench into everything I've worked for here."

Dax shrugged. "I sort of doubt she'll come here. She'll be pissed off at us all, sure, but I don't think she wants to run into her brothers. It's been a long time since she left. She could've come back anytime she wanted. She hasn't, so she didn't want to. What will happen is that she will nag us into coming back to Maine for holidays."

"She's always been so close mouthed about what happened with her brothers. Don't you wonder what happened?"

"Sure, I do. In all the time you've been here, has no one in that family ever mentioned their long-lost sister?"

Marc shook his head. "Nope. No long-lost sister story has ever been told to me."

"Hmm, I wonder if they've just forgotten her. You know, wrote her out of their lives and never gave her a thought."

Marc shrugged. "I don't know. I can't imagine every forgetting Sami."

"I can't either," Dax said. "Sami is impossible to forget."

"And you think our mother is possible to forget?"

Dax shook his head. "Gosh, no. She's the most remarkable woman ever born."

"My point exactly. How could her brothers not find her? How could they not hire private investigators and search the entire country for her? It's not like she moved to Antarctica. She's been in Maine for decades."

"Well, Maine is a good distance from Texas," Marc said.

"True, but still..."

"And she does have a different last name."

"But the Montgomerys have the money to track her down, if they wanted to. I mean, she couldn't hide if a PI wanted to find her."

"I don't think she's trying to hide. I think..." Dax yawned. "I don't know what I think about Mom, but I do know what I think about me. I think I'm going to bed."

Marc laughed. "Me, too. Tomorrow is Monday, which means I get to go through all the weekend reports. Plus, I've got an early morning joint task force meeting."

"Yeah, what's going on that needs a joint task force?"

"We've had some cattle rustling in the area."

Dax said, "I know. It's crazy to think that in this day and age, people still rustle cows."

"Oh, you have no idea. Wait, how did you know we had a problem?"

"Travis mentioned it the day we met. That's why he was out riding the fence line. Speaking of which, I'm surprised I never heard from him or his wife. He sounded so certain about inviting us out to their place."

Marc's face reddened and he shifted his gaze toward the wall. "We sort of have."

Dax frowned. "What do you mean?"

"Caroline, that's his wife, called last night and invited us to dinner."

"Really? And you didn't think that was important enough to mention to me?"

"How am I going to take you and Sami to dinner with Travis and Caroline? How am I going to explain her? She looks just like Mom. You think no one will notice?

Dax shook his head. "No, they won't know. I doubt neither Caroline nor Travis has ever seen a picture of Mom. How would they know?"

Marc nodded. "Valid point. I'll reach out to Caroline or Travis, and maybe we'll just go by for drinks."

"No, not good enough. I would really like to get

to know them. If I'm going to live here, I need to learn how to avoid the landmines."

"Wait." Marc turned toward him. "You've going to live here?"

Dax shrugged. "I don't know. I like it. The area's pretty. Texas is certainly unique."

His brother laughed. "Texas is definitely unique. They do have their own little country down here."

"Plus, if you and Sami are here, I want to be here too. But I still have to figure what I'm going to do for a job. I mean, there is only so much I can do with this. It can limit my activities." He tapped his artificial leg. "I mean, it's not like I can be a lineman for the county."

Marc laughed. "Yeah, I don't believe you'll be doing that."

"Anyway, we can talk more about this later." He stretched. "I heard my bed calling my name."

Sometime in the middle of the night, Dax was doing his usual not sleeping when his cell phone buzzed and lit up. How very odd. Very few people had his number, and even fewer would call him at this hour. His mind went to his parents and he snatched the phone off the table. The area code was 501, followed by a number he didn't recognize.

"Hello?"

"Is this Major Dax Cooper?" a female voice asked.

"It is."

"I'm so sorry for calling at such an awful hour, but I didn't feel this could wait."

Dax frowned at the urgency in the woman's voice. "What couldn't wait?" He swung his legs off the bed and reached for his artificial leg to put it on.

"This is Marjorie Stephens, David Stephens's mother."

"Oh, yes, Mrs. Stephens. What's wrong?" He waited for her to say that Captain Stephens had died. His brain cancer had been terminal when Dax had sent his friend back home from Afghanistan. There'd been nothing medically that could be done for him, so he'd essentially sent him to die surrounded by his family instead of dirt and hostiles.

"I'm sorry. I woke you. I should've waited a little later to call."

"I was up. What can do I for you, Mrs. Stephens?"

"It's Davey. The doctors have put him in hospice care."

"I'm so sorry." And he was sorry, but he wasn't sure why he was the one being called.

"Thank you, Major. We've known this was coming, but..." She sniffed. "I don't think there is really any way to prepare to lose your child."

"I'm sure you're right. Is there something I can do?"

"Davey has asked to see you. Would it be possible for you to fly here? Today? We will, of course, pay for everything."

"Where are you?"

"Northwest Arkansas, and you're in Maine?"

"No, I'm in the Dallas area visiting family."

"Perfect. There are a number of direct flights from Dallas to Bentonville. This would mean everything to us, Major. Please come."

He scrubbed his hand down his face. "Sure."

"We are talking on my cell phone. Send me your flight information when you have it, and I'll have a car waiting for you at the airport."

Dax was in the air by nine a.m. He realized by nine-thirty that he'd left his cell phone in the kitchen when he'd set it down to leave Marc a note. No big deal. This was a quick trip. He'd probably be back this evening.

Six

Monday morning, Cori woke with a smile. Last night had been great. She was tickled, and more than a little flattered, that Dax had remembered what she'd said about astronomy with her dad. Plus, his apology and sexy good-night kiss had made her glad she'd given him a second chance.

The aroma of brewing coffee pulled her from the sheets. It was such a hassle to set up the pot and timer at night, but so worth the effort the next morning. As she poured her first cup of the day, she wondered if Dax would call or text today. He said he'd call. He just hadn't said when. But even if she didn't hear from him today, they had made dinner plans for this weekend. At some point this week, they'd talk.

Monday passed like so many Mondays. She took on a couple of new cases, even though her schedule was already bulging. Even though she got irritated with herself, she couldn't help but check for messages or texts from Dax between clients. Her phone remained silent.

Tuesday was a repeat of Monday, minus the new cases. On the drive home, Cori debated reaching out to Dax. After all, this was the twenty-first century. A woman didn't have to sit around and wait for a guy to call or text. Women should feel comfortable going after what they wanted, so why didn't she feel that way too? Her internal battle of call-him/-don't-call-him played in her brain until she was sick of herself.

After stripping out of her nice work clothes, she dressed in shorts, a T-shirt, and sneakers and headed to her front yard to pull weeds from her flower beds. Ridding her beds of the invasive weeds was cathartic. She was sure there was a metaphor or psychological meaning in the pleasure she got from the action, but for today, it was a way to relieve stress. Mother Nature was firing up the burners to give Texas its usual fiery weather for the summer. Now was the perfect time to get her inpatients and begonias established so she could enjoy their flowers through the hot summer months.

Standing, she stretched her back and studied her handiwork. A pile of wilted greenery lay outside her bed border and inside, clean areas were ready for planting. She smiled, pleased with her handiwork. She'd be able to finish the project this weekend regardless of whether she and Dax went out on Friday or Saturday. Speaking of which...She retrieved her phone from the porch and checked for a call or message. There'd been calls, all from her mother.

Nothing from Dax. While she would have loved to hear from him, they'd only had a couple of dates. She didn't think he was the type who would ghost her. Most likely, he was simply busy getting settled.

After a healthy mental debate, she sent him a text.

Cori: *Hey! It's me. I'm trying to get my weekend plans in order. I wasn't sure which night you planned for us to have dinner. Either works for me. Let me know. Hope everything is going well.*

She waited for a reply. Nothing came or hadn't by the time her eyelids finally closed.

Wednesday morning came early, or so it seemed. Her night had been comprised of tossing and turning. A couple of years ago, she'd bought a mattress that allowed her to adjust the sleep pressure and temperature. All the literature had promised she'd sleep like a baby, and most nights, she did. However, if the mattress brochure was accurate, she'd been a colicky baby all night. Her alarm was more welcome than usual. At least her night of being a rotisserie chicken was over.

She dragged herself to the kitchen and slugged down a cup of strong, black coffee. Her phone had been on silent all night, so if a text from Dax had come through, she wouldn't have heard it. She unplugged the phone from the charger and checked texts and phone calls. Nothing.

As she poured her second cup, she suspected there would be numerous cups of coffee in her day, which did not bode well for her. She was scheduled to be in court at ten this morning to give testimony in an acrimonious divorce where the two young children were being used as pawns on both sides. She hated these cases and tried to avoid them as much as possible. However, her friend and lawyer, KC Montgomery, had asked her to take on this case as a favor, and she had. Her testimony was ready. Now, she only had to get her body ready.

Since she didn't have to be at the courthouse until nine-thirty, she ran by her office to review her files. As she was walking into her office, she heard her assistant on the phone.

"Okay. Sure. I've got it. No, no. I've got her schedule in front of me. Next month should be fine. I'll pencil it in."

Cori stood in front of her assistant's desk with an arched brow. "Something I should know?"

"No court today," she said. "The judge had to have emergency surgery, and the case was continued until next month."

Cori shook her head. "I know it's not the judge's fault, but those poor kids will be pulled back and forth between their parents for another month."

Her assistant tsked. "What is wrong with people, using their children like a tug toy between two dogs." She sighed. "Since we had no idea how long court would take today, you have nothing else on your schedule today."

"Yay, paperwork day," Cori said sarcastically.

"You need me to do anything to help?"

"Pull all the files for the past week. Do I have all the files for appointments this week?"

Her assistant nodded and then snapped her fingers. "You have a message. Duh, sorry. It skipped my mind."

A wave of nervous excitement rushed through Cori's system. Dax!

Her excitement came to a crashing fall when she saw the note was from another referral from social services. She'd call the social worker back, and then she might sneak off for the rest of the day. Today looked like a great day to do some flower planting.

After working for a couple of hours, her stomach reminded her that she'd skipped breakfast. Cori stretched her arms over her head and stood. The sun was high in the sky, but a low front had brought in mid-seventies weather.

"I'm headed down to Heavenly Delights Bakery for lunch. Want anything?" Cori asked her assistant as she slipped her purse over her shoulder.

"Yes, please. Porchia makes these chocolate-filled pastries. I'd love one of those."

"Sure. I'll be back later." Cori tapped her purse. "I have my phone if you need to reach me before I return."

The walk from her office to Porchia's Heavenly Delights was only a ten-minute walk usually. However, the weather was too perfect to hurry from one building to another. Cori slowed down as she strolled past the courthouse and around downtown Whispering Springs square. Sure, she could have put her office in one of the newer office buildings going up or even in a residential house turned commercial property. Any other place would probably have been cheaper and definitely newer. However, a couple of years ago, downtown Whispering Springs had undergone a total renovation. Old buildings had been gutted and renovated. Murals depicting Whispering Springs's past now gleamed from brick walls. Sidewalks, once broken and uneven, were new and level. Walking in the area was like taking a deep breath of fresh air after being in a smoke-filled room.

Porchia's bakery was busy, not that Cori was surprised. Heavenly Delights Bakery had expanded into simple lunches...sandwiches, soups, and a daily special. During the downtown renovation, Porchia and her husband, Darren, had taken over the building next door, knocking out an opening in the wall to join the two spaces. Since the building and menu expansion, business had been rocking...like today. The line to order was out the door.

As she considered leaving, someone slipped an arm through hers and whispered, "I know the back way in."

She turned toward the voice. Magda Hobbs Montgomery stood beside her with a wide grin. "Magda! Long time no see."

Magda returned the smile. "Ditto. Come on. Sisters-in-law have privileges."

"But I'm not a sister-in-law."

"You're with one, however. Come on."

Magda tugged Cori down the street and around the corner. There, a high fence protected a group of parked cars. "Employee parking," she explained, as she punched in a code and the gate slid open. Once they were inside the enclosure, the gate closed. "Ever since Porchia had that stalker a few years back, Darren put up the safety fence. Each employee has their own code to enter. Once they leave employment, their code is erased, and voila! No more entry." She grinned. "I have my own code."

She led them to a back door and let them inside. They walked into the kitchen, which was in full swing. People talking, plates banging, and steam rising from the stove and ovens.

"Hi, gang," Magda shouted over the din. "This is Cori."

"Hi, Cori," the group called and went back to work.

Cori shook her head in amusement. "I've missed you," she said to Magda. "Ever since you married Reno, we hardly get to spend time together."

Magda nodded. "You should come to Montgomery wives' night, and before you protest you aren't a Montgomery wife, there are usually some friends who join us." As she spoke, she led them to a LED monitor in the corner. "What do you want to eat?"

"A sandwich maybe?"

"Bruno," Magda called across the kitchen. "What's today's special?"

"Meatloaf, mashed potatoes, lima beans, with a yeast roll."

"Yum. I'm having that," Magda said, punching in the order.

"Make it two," Cori said.

"Got it." Magda entered the order on the screen. "Okay, let's see if we can find a table."

"Wait. I need to pay."

Magda waved her off. "My treat. I have a running tab. And don't worry. Porchia will send a bill. She always does."

They found a small table inside the expanded area and sat.

"So, fill me in," Magda said. "Tell me all about Dax Cooper. Does he kiss good? What's he like in bed?" Magda propped her elbows and rested her head in her hands. "Take pity on this old married woman who needs to live the single life through you."

Cori laughed. "How did you know I went out with Dax Cooper?"

Magda rolled her eyes. "You're kidding. Whispering Springs gossip vine, of course. Plus, KC saw you at Rick's on the River."

"Well..."

Before Cori could continue, Porchia came from the kitchen with two plates. "Princess Magda of Montgomery and Princess Cora Belle of Lambert?"

Cori flashed her gaze toward Magda, who was laughing as she waved at her sister-in-law.

"Seriously?" Porchia said as she set the loaded plates on the table. She dragged up an extra chair. "Princesses?" Then she laughed as she reached over and put her hand on Cori's arm. "Good to see you, Cori. It's been a while."

Cori nodded. "I know. I swear every day that I'm

going to get down here for lunch, and something always comes up." She glanced around. "Looks like business is going well."

"It is. I've had to hire five new people just to handle the lunch crowd. But I didn't come over to talk about me. I want to hear about your date with Dax Cooper." She grinned. "KC can't keep a secret unless it's something legal. So, spill everything."

While she and Magda ate and Porchia drank a glass of iced tea, Cori told them about the dinner date on Friday and the picnic-slash-stargazing on Sunday.

"And his kisses?" Magda asked before taking a gulp of water.

Cori sighed. "Really, really good." Pressing a hand to her stomach, which had butterflies at the memory, she added, "I do believe the man has had a lot of practice."

Porchia chuckled. "When are you seeing him again?"

Cori took a large bite of meatloaf to delay having to reply. She pointed to her mouth, as in I-can't-answer-right-now.

"I'm here all day," Porchia said. "I can wait."

"I don't have anywhere to be," Magda replied. "I also can wait you out."

Cori sighed. "I hate both of you."

Porchia slid her chair closer and put her arm around Cori's shoulder. "He ghosted you?" She looked at Magda. "Have Reno beat him up, okay?"

Before Magda and Reno married, he'd torn a guy apart who'd messed with Magda.

"Stop it," Cori said. "We're supposed to go out this weekend, but I haven't heard from him."

"You're the one who always advises her clients to take control of their lives and not to let life control them, right? Take your own advice," Porchia said. "Take control of the situation. Text him, or better yet, call him."

Cori's appetite suddenly evaporated. She pushed her plate forward. "I did. Last night. He didn't respond."

"Maybe something's wrong," Magda suggested. "He's Marc Singer's brother, right? Call Marc."

Cori was aghast at the suggestion. "There's taking control of one's life and reaching out, and then there's stalking. It can be a fine line, so no. I'm not calling his brother. How embarrassing." She put an imaginary phone to her face. "Hello, Sheriff Singer? This is a woman who went out with your brother twice, and now he's not calling me. Can you make him call me?" She dropped her hand. "Um, no."

"I can get Reno to call the sheriff, just friendly like. He can ask him about his brother," Magda said.

Cori smiled and reached across the table to touch her friend's hand. "Thank you, but don't do that. I'm sure I'll hear from Dax soon."

"Good. After the next date, you can come to Montgomery women's night out and tell us everything." Porchia tapped her knuckles on the table. "And we'll want all the details, right, Magda?"

"Oh, absolutely."

After lunch, Cori returned to her office, but she

was restless to work. Finally, at three, she left for the day and went to the Garden of Eden nursery to pick up bedding plants. She felt like getting her hands dirty.

With the bedding plants in the ground and no weeds left to pull, Cori headed inside to shower. She didn't want to check her phone for messages, but she had no control over her hands, which picked up her phone and scrolled. There was one phone message from her mom.

"Hi, honey. It's mom calling to invite you to dinner on Friday night. Elsie Belle is coming to town for the weekend. Oscar is out of town again. So, we'll see you Friday about six, okay? I'd love to have you stay the weekend too. It'd be like old times. The whole family back together. Talk to you later."

Old times? The last thing Cori wanted was old times. Sandwiched between two beautiful sisters, she couldn't help but compare herself, and she always came up lacking.

Interesting that Oscar was out of town again. Her sister, Elsie, had married Oscar Billings in a lavish, over-the-top wedding two years ago. It was Elsie's first marriage and Oscar's third. He was a tad older than Elsie, forty-eight to her sister's thirty-six, but who was she to judge whom her sister loved? She simply couldn't see what Elsie saw in him—other than his billions of dollars.

Friday night dinner. Should she send Dax another text about not being available on Friday for dinner? She had told him both nights were open. Maybe she should, although she wished their dinner was Friday so she'd have a valid reason to bail on her family.

Cori: *Hey! It's me again. I have a family thing to do on Friday, so I was hoping Saturday would work for you for dinner. Talk soon.*

She put her phone on the charger and headed for the shower, confident there'd be a reply text shortly.

There wasn't.

When she settled into bed that night, saying she was disappointed would've been the understatement of the day. She was downright crushed by Dax's lack of response.

Was Dax ghosting her? The thought made her stomach churn and her heart fall to her knees. Sunday night had been magical under the stars, but was it possible she was the only one who'd felt that?

Seven

～～

Thursday and Friday passed without a word from Dax. She'd already sent two text messages, but she'd be damned before she would call him.

Friday night, she headed to her parents' ranch, and no, she didn't pack a bag. She had no intention of staying the night. She loved her family, but she loved her privacy more.

She was met at her car door by Fisher, her parents' golden retriever.

"Hey, boy," she said, stepping from her car to give Fisher some head rubs. "Am I the last one here?"

"Yes," came the reply from the porch.

She looked up and found her sister, Elsie, sitting in the rocker, a martini glass in her hand.

"I see you've started the drinking without me," Cori said as she climbed the steps.

"What can I say? It was a long day of shopping."

Cori sat in the second rocker beside Elsie. "Shopping for anything in particular or just wandering the shops looking for something to buy?"

Elsie shrugged. "Trying to help Annabelle find a dress for prom."

"Why? Can't she find one herself?"

Elsie gestured toward the pitcher on the table. "Help yourself to a martini, if you want one. I made a batch for the evening."

Cori poured herself a drink. "What's going on? You seem, I don't know, a little depressed."

Her older sister sighed. "Trying to make lemonade."

Cori got the reference. Their grandmother always tried to find the positive in every situation. She'd always told them that when life handed you a bushel of lemons, make enough lemonade for the town.

"Want to talk about your lemons?" Cori heard her professional tone, which was much like the one she used with clients.

Apparently, so did her sister since she turned and glared at her. "Am I on the clock or is this a freebie?"

Cori sighed. "Do you want to be on the clock?"

"No, I want to talk to my sister, not Dr. Lambert."

Cori mimicked removing a hat and placing it on the floor. Then she took a gulp of cold vodka martini. "I'm ready."

Elsie chuckled, but to Cori's ears, it didn't sound all that happy.

"I didn't think marriage would be like this," Elsie said.

"Like what?"

"Me, alone so much. I knew Oscar traveled for business, but I guess I didn't realize how much."

"So, go with him. It's not like there's anything keeping you in Texas."

"He doesn't want me to."

"Hmm. Did he say why?"

"Just that I'd be in the way."

"Yikes. That's kind of mean."

"Yeah, I thought so too. Plus..." Elsie looked at Cori, her eyes glassy with unshed tears. "I don't want mom to know any of this, okay?"

Cori nodded. "Okay."

"When we got engaged, he promised we could have kids. Now..." Elsie shrugged and took a gulp from her martini glass. "Now, he says he doesn't want any. Never has and never will."

"I'm sorry." And she was. Not that she thought her sister would be a wonderful mother, but because she hated seeing anyone so dejected. "Maybe he'll change his mind in a year or so."

Elsie shook her head. "We've been married over two years and every year, he's more adamant on the no-children-ever stand."

"So, what are you going to do?"

"There's more." Her sister sighed heavily. "I think there's someone else."

Cori's mouth sagged. "As in he has a girlfriend?"

Elsie shrugged. "I think so. Do you think I should hire a PI and have him followed?"

"I know you had a prenup. Is there anything in there about being unfaithful?"

"Yeah, for me. At the time, I didn't notice there's nothing in there about him being unfaithful."

"I'm not a lawyer, Elsie, but I think you should see one. Go see KC Montgomery. Get her advice."

"No way. It'd be all Whispering Springs that I wasn't enough for my husband, so he had to get a girlfriend. I'd rather not be the subject of gossip."

"Don't blame you. You want me to pretend I have a client looking for a divorce shark and get some Dallas names?"

Elsie reached over and grabbed Cori's hand. "You'd do that for me?"

"Of course. You'd do it for me if I needed you to." They both knew that was a lie. Elsie was the star of her universe. Everyone else a circling planet.

"Elsie, honey, have you seen—Oh, you're here," Clover Lamber said to Cori. "I was beginning to worry. I hope you brought a bag."

Not in the mood to handle a sleepover discussion, Cori smiled. "I'm starved," she lied. "When's dinner?"

"We're waiting on Annabelle and her date to get here."

"Do you need help in the kitchen?" Cori asked as she began to rise from her chair.

"No, no. Sit down. Everything is under control." Her mother stared off into the distance. "I've been seeing a truck over at the Hanson old place. I wonder what is going on."

"It's for sale," Cori said. "I suppose prospective buyers are looking at it."

"Hmm. I hope we get some good neighbors."

Cori started to say something about Sheriff Singer looking at the property, but her mother did love to be on the starting end of gossip. So, Cori thought it best to keep that to herself.

A red and black truck turned off the main road and headed up the Lambert drive.

"That's probably Annabelle and Noah now. I'll let Cook know so she can get the bread in the oven."

Their mother hurried back inside as Elsie refilled both glasses.

"Noah, as in Noah Graham, Caroline's little brother?"

Elsie chuckled. "Not so little anymore. When was the last time you saw him?"

"Gosh, when he was fifteen or so." She didn't add that Noah had been one of her troubled teens back in the day. His sister, Caroline, and his brother-in-law, Travis Montgomery, had plopped him in her office and told him to get straight or else. He'd gotten his head screwed back on and pulled up his grades. It hadn't taken much on her part to help him find his way.

"Well, you're in for a surprise," Elsie said with a snort. "That scrawny kid grew up and, well, you'll see."

The truck parked and their younger sister leaped from the seat. "Hey, y'all," she yelled.

Elsie and Cori waved.

Out of the driver's side stepped a tall, muscular young man with tousled brown hair with sun-bleached gold streaks. His face was angular, and with his wide smile, he was astonishingly handsome.

"Holy shit," Cori whispered. "God didn't make them like that when I was in high school."

Elsie chuckled. "No kidding, and if he had, I swear I would've gone sans underwear to school every day."

Cori snorted.

Annabelle grabbed her date's hand and pulled him up onto the porch. "These are my sisters. You probably know them. This is Elsie Belle and Cora Belle, but we all call her Cori. Y'all, this is Noah Graham"

Cori waited to see if Noah would acknowledge knowing her.

He smiled at both of them. His smile was deadly, and Cori would have beat her last dollar it got him into more girls' pants than she was comfortable thinking about.

"I know your sister. Dr. Lambert, nice to see you again." He held out his hand.

Cori shook his hand and said, "It's just Cori. Good to see you again, Noah. Staying out of trouble, I hope."

He laughed. "Yes, ma'am." He turned to Elsie. "We've met, but I'm sure you don't remember."

Elsie gave him what Cori thought of as her sultry laugh. "Sure, I do, Noah. It's nice to see you again."

Their mother opened the door and stepped onto

the porch. "Hello, Noah. Nice to see you. Congratulations on getting into Harvard."

"Thank you, Mrs. Lambert. I haven't decided if I'm going there or going to Austin. I'm still debating."

"Oh, you can't *not* go," Mrs. Lambert said. "It's the opportunity of a lifetime."

Noah glanced at Annabelle, who was clinging to his hand like a lifeline. "I'm sure it is, but my friends and family are here. I think staying close to home would be good too."

Cori was sure her mother wanted Noah as far away from Annabelle as possible. There was a look in their eyes that suggested more than friendship.

"Well, come on in," Clover said. "Dinner is ready, and Cori said she was starving."

Cori frowned. "I did?"

"You did," her mother said. "Come on, now. Let's eat."

Clover held open the door for her daughters and Noah. They trooped to the dining room, where food waited in serving dishes on the sideboard.

"All my girls are home," Dale Lambert boomed as he entered the room.

"Hi, Daddy," Cori said and hurried over to give her dad a hug.

"Hi, honey." He hugged her tight. "You lost some weight?"

Elsie snickered at the question.

Cori shot her a hateful glare. "I haven't, but thanks for thinking that."

"Okay, grab a plate and fill it up," Clover ordered. "Guests first," she said to her husband.

"She means you," Annabelle said to Noah. Then, still holding tight to his hand, she led him over to the sideboard. There, she began to uncover the various dishes. The room filled with delicious aromas from the beef roast, roasted new potatoes, green bean almandine, baby carrots, and grilled asparagus.

"I'll get the rolls from the kitchen while y'all fill your plates," Clover said as she left.

Once they were seated around the table, Annabelle said, "Noah and I have some news."

Everyone immediately stopped.

Dale set his fork down and looked at his youngest daughter.

Cori's heart skittered out of fear the Annabelle was skipping college to get married.

Her mother's face went pale.

Elsie paused and then lifted her martini glass to her lips. "This should be interesting," she said. "You have our attention, so what's the big news?" She tapped a long fingernail against the stem of the glass.

Annabelle was almost bouncing in her chair with excitement. She looked at Noah and then back at her family. "Noah and I got elected Prom King and Queen today."

Cori and her parents released held breaths.

Elsie nodded. "I remember being prom queen my senior year. Remember, Cori?"

"Sure." Of course, Cori remembered. She hadn't been prom queen nor part of the court her senior year. And while Elsie probably didn't mean to rub salt in those wounds, Cori couldn't help but still feel a tad inadequate in the looks department.

"Y'all still have the princesses and princes' court?" Elsie asked.

Annabelle nodded. "The cool thing is all my friends got princess status. This is going to be the best prom ever." She looked at their mom. "And that's why I need a new dress."

Clover groaned. "You already have your dress for prom."

"But that was before I was named queen. That dress will never work now."

"Don't worry," Elsie said. "I've got you. We'll go shopping in Dallas tomorrow. I know exactly where to take you."

"I'll clear my day and go too," Clover said. "We do have to stay within a budget."

"Mom," Annabelle whined, clearly not wanting her mom to go. With their mom along, there'd be no sexy dress with a plunging neckline, something Cori was sure Elsie would pick out.

"We'll all go. You, Elsie, me, and Cori—the Lambert women go shopping."

Cori couldn't think of a more miserable way to spend a Saturday, unless it was locked in an office with a stack of files. Nope, tomorrow she was going to be in her yard doing something. She wasn't going to spend it going to expensive dress shops.

"Thanks, but no thanks," Cori said.

"Aww, come on," her mom said, "We'll have fun."

"Y'all have fun without me," Cori replied. "I already have plans." And those plans did not include shopping, her most detested activity.

Her mother started to object again when Cori's phone rang. Clover's eyes flashed. "You know we don't allow phones at the dinner table."

Cori held up one finger. "Hello?"

"Cori? This is Marc Singer."

"Sheriff Singer, what can I do for you?" Cori stood and walked away from the table, her heart in her throat. If the sheriff was calling her, it must be about Dax, and it could only be bad news. He'd been in an accident. He'd left the state. He was dead. It had to be horrible if she was getting a call.

"I owe you an apology," Sheriff Singer said.

Cori opened the front door and stepped onto the porch for privacy. "Okay, why?"

"My brother is going to have my head," he said with a groan. "Dax had to leave town on Monday, sort of an emergency trip. He accidentally left his cell phone here. He called me on Monday night and asked me to get in touch with you and let you know that he would be back, but probably not until next week, and he would have to reschedule your date for this weekend. I said I would, and then it completely skipped my brain." He sighed loudly. "I had one of those weeks, but that's no excuse. I'm sorry. You must have had terrible thoughts about Dax all week."

"Well, I confess to being a little concerned we hadn't confirmed our dinner plans, but I understand how these things happen. I appreciate your letting me know. Would it be too nosey to ask what kind of emergency?"

"One of the guys who was under his command was put on hospice. Apparently, Dax and this guy had gotten to be friends. Anyway, his last request to his family was to speak with Dax, so the family flew Dax to their hometown."

"Oh, that's so sad. I'm sorry."

"Yeah, Dax said the soldier had been diagnosed with a brain tumor while stationed in Afghanistan. Turned out, it was a fatal form of brain cancer. Nothing could be done, but at least he got to spend some time with his family before the end."

"I'm glad Dax went then."

"Yeah, so anyway, I screwed up and forgot to call, and that's all on me, not my brother."

"Thanks, Sheriff. I understand the pressures of the job, but I do appreciate the call."

"Dax will call when he gets back, and Cori...?"

"Yeah?"

"If you're going to be dating my brother, you should probably call me Marc."

The front door opened and her mother stepped onto the porch. "Is everything all right?" she mouthed.

"Thanks, again, Marc. I'll be sure to do that."

As soon as she clicked off the phone, her mother asked again, "Everything okay?"

"It's fine. The sheriff was relaying a message to me."

"From his brother?"

Cori's eyes widened. "You knew the guy you set me up on a blind date with was the sheriff's brother?"

"Someone might have mentioned it to me."

Cori shook her head. "Damn. Does this town not understand how to keep a secret?"

Her mom chuckled. "Apparently not. After dinner, I want you to tell me all about Dax Cooper."

With a groan, Cori asked, "Can't a girl have any secrets from her mother?"

"Of course not. I want to hear all about the sheriff's mysterious brother. The rumor mill has been churning for a month about him. Now, let's go finish dinner. When I left, Elsie was explaining to Noah why he needs a tux for the prom, not just a suit."

Cori laughed. "She does love to tell everyone else what to do, doesn't she?"

"That she does."

"And I'd suggest you give the two of them a firm budget for that dress. You know Elsie only buys the most expensive."

Her mother rolled her eyes. "Don't I know it. Now, let's go finish dinner so we can gossip, er, talk afterward."

Cori followed her mother back into the house, not yet mentioning that she would be going home tonight. If she told her mom now, they'd argue about why she was going home and then they'd rehash the entire argument again when she left. Better to wait and have that discussion only once.

"Okay, then. It's all settled," Elsie was saying as Cori and her mom retook their seats. "I'll call Travis and tell him that you must have a tux for next weekend."

Given Elsie's history with Travis, and knowing his wife, Caroline, wasn't Elsie's biggest fan, Cori said, "I think Noah can handle his own business, Elsie. Calling Travis isn't necessary, I don't think." When Elsie glared at her, Cori arched a brow, clearly conveying that calling Travis was a horrible idea.

"Fine," Elsie said with a huff.

As soon as dinner was over, Annabelle and Noah were out the door like fired bullets. Cori longed to follow as quickly, but instead, she hung around and helped carry the dishes to the kitchen. She hoped to get Elsie alone again to find out what was going on with Oscar, but no such luck. Their mother wasn't letting the two of them out of her sight.

The evening ended much as Cori had known it would...with her going home, deaf to her mother's pleas to spend the night. The total drive time from the ranch to Cori's house was a little over thirty minutes, so to her mind, it made no logical sense to stay. Plus, she wanted nothing to do with the prom dress shopping in the morning. She didn't need another reminder that she hadn't been as popular in high school as her sisters, not that she held any resentment, no matter what her own therapist said.

Saturday morning, the sun was bright and the weather ideal for outside work. She'd put off scrubbing her porch as she hated the job, but with summer just around the corner, she knew she'd spend a lot of time out here.

She changed into an old pair of sweats that'd been cut off mid-thigh, not that she'd wanted them that short, but a mid-thigh hole had dictated the length. She paired those with an old, and also holey, SMU T-shirt that she didn't know where she'd gotten. Bare-foot was the order of the day since no matter the shoe, it'd be wet quickly.

Armed with a bucket of soapy water, rags, mop, broom, and window cleaner, she tackled the grime winter had left behind. She worked from top to bottom, meaning water, clean and dirty, dripped on her head.

It was close to noon when she finished scrubbing the porch floor. Her hair hung in her face in damp ringlets. The T-shirt and sweat shorts were a few stages beyond damp, but her windows shone and her furniture gleamed. Since she was already dirty and wet, the window beyond the porch could also use some cleaning, but she deserved a break before moving over there.

She dropped into her porch swing and blew out a satisfied smile, maybe the last one for the day. As she watched, a yellow, low-slung sports car pulled into her drive and parked. Her brow furrowed as she tried to figure out who she knew that drove that distinctives car, but no one came to mind.

The driver's door opened, and a tall, handsome blond man stepped out of the car and back into her life after walking away ten years ago.

"Hello, Ree," he said. "It's been a long time."

Greg Simmons, her college boyfriend, and the

man she'd been engaged to, smiled at her. Her heart skipped. Her breath swooshed from her lungs. Her stomach flipped so fast she was momentarily nauseated. Greg was the only person in the world who shortened her name from Cori to just Ree.

Cori stood on wobbly legs and stared.

Greg chuckled and walked toward her. "I guess you're a little surprised to see me."

She nodded. "Yeah, surprised is one word. What are you doing here?"

He stopped at the bottom of her steps and looked up at her. "Leaving you was the worst mistake of my life. I've come to win you back."

Eight

Dax had been surprised by the early wake-up call from David Stephen's mother. The time between the phone call and the plane's departure from DFW had been short. But the military had taught him to how to move quickly when necessary, and that conversation had put him in the "move it" mode.

He'd barely gotten settled into his first-class seat when the attendants closed the door for departure. Sometimes, he felt as if during his career, he'd had as much airtime as sleep hours. The attractive brunette attendant lifted the receiver next to the door and began to speak.

"Welcome to American Airlines Flight 786 to Bentonville, Arkansas. At this time, the captain requests that all electronic devices be discontinued or put into airplane mode."

As she was speaking, Dax patted his pockets looking for his cell phone. He came up empty-handed. He remembered having the phone when he'd left the note for Marc. Dammit. It was probably still sitting on the kitchen counter. Well, hell. Of course, it probably was a moot point. There was a good chance this was an up-and-back trip today.

Upon landing, he was met by a man dressed in a chauffeur's uniform holding up a sign that read, "Major Cooper."

"I'm Dax Cooper," he said to the man.

"Excellent. I'm Joseph, the Stephens's driver. Do you have luggage I need to retrieve?"

Dax shook his head. "Just this duffle bag."

"I'll take that," Joseph said, reaching for the bag

Normally, Dax would have argued, but he handed over the bag. His leg was bothering him some today, and handing over the bag gave him a little relief.

"This way, then," Joseph said, and began walking toward the exit.

Joseph was a man of few words. After opening the rear door of a black Mercedes sedan, he stored Dax's duffle bag in the trunk.

"We have a little bit of a drive," Joseph said as he slipped behind the wheel.

Dax slipped on his sunglasses and settled into the soft leather seats. A thirty-minute drive later, the sedan pulled up to a gated estate. The driver punched in a code, the gate slowly swung open, and they proceeded up the drive to a massive, modern, rock and glass mansion. Dax tried to remember if he'd known that Stephens had come from money, but mostly, he'd seemed like a good old boy from Arkansas.

As the car pulled to a stop, the front door to the manor opened, and an attractive blonde stepped onto the rock landing. Dax stepped from the car as Joseph retrieved his duffle from the truck.

"Major Cooper?" the woman asked.

"It's just Dax now, ma'am."

She nodded. "I'm Marjorie Stephens, David's mother. Thank you for coming."

Dax shook the hand she extended. "Mrs. Stephens. It's nice to meet you, but I'd rather it was under better circumstances."

"Marjorie, please. I know coming here so suddenly was an inconvenience, so I want you to know how much my husband and I appreciate your kindness. Please, come in." She looked toward Joseph and said, "Put the major's luggage in the guest house, please."

The chauffeur nodded and headed around the side of the house.

"I thought you'd be more comfortable with your own space," she said as they walked inside.

The entry rose two levels, giving the house an open, airy feel. The wooden floors gleamed. Expensive-looking paintings were displayed on walls, each with its own special lighting. A baby grand piano occupied the corner of a large gathering room. Dax only got glances of other rooms as he followed Marjorie Stephens through her house toward a wing that jutted north from the main residence.

"When we built this house," Marjorie said, "we added a wing for David so he would have his own space. We'd hoped the day would come when he would marry and bring his family here." She looked over at Dax. "You know the saying 'Man plans, God laughs?'" She shrugged. "Sadly, that's our story."

Her voice was sad but resigned to what was coming, or that's how it sounded to Dax's ears.

"I promised David I'd bring you straight to his room when you arrived, but you should prepare yourself." She stopped at the entrance to the wing expansion and gestured around. "As you probably deduced, we can afford the best treatment for David's condition, and we have tried everything medically possible for his cancer, but glioblastoma doesn't really have a treatment. We've been able to extend his life for these eighteen months, but only to give him, and us, some time together. He's lost probably fifty pounds since you've seen him, as well as his hair. So, the man you sent home to his family looks vastly different from the man you knew."

Dax nodded. "I understand. Are there any subjects I shouldn't discuss with him?"

Marjorie shook her head. "No, not really. He likes to talk about the past and his life. We usually let him lead the conversation."

"Okay. I'd like to see him."

Marjorie walked him down a hall that opened into an area that'd been designed to look like a separate house with its own living room, kitchen, and multiple bedrooms and baths. She led him through the living room to a door at the end of the hall. She paused, and then knocked before opening the door.

"David? Major Cooper is here," she said as they entered.

A woman in scrubs stood beside the bed. "Good afternoon, Mrs. Stephens," the woman said.

"Hello, Julia. This is Dax Cooper, David's military friend. Dax, this is Julia, David's daytime nurse."

"I'll just step outside and give you some privacy," Julia said and left.

The man in the bed was David Stephens, but Dax was glad Marjorie had warned him about David's appearance. He resembled the man Dax used to know, but David was a shadow of his former self. Thin and gaunt, his skin had taken on an ashy unhealthy pallor. His face lacked any color. He reminded Dax of actors in vampire shows. Laying in the bed, it's head on David's leg was a golden retriever.

But then David smiled, and he transformed into the man Dax had known and worked with for many years.

"Dax," David said, his voice weak, "you came."

Dax snorted. "Man, did I have a choice? You had your mom call, and what could I do but drop everything and fly here? It's not like I've got a life."

David laughed. "Sit," he said and gestured toward a comfortable-looking wingback chair beside the bed. "I want to hear everything. Show me your leg."

Marjorie quietly left the room as Dax dropped into the chair.

"Man, let me tell you about this sexy nurse I had in rehab," Dax began. There'd been no sexy nurse, or if there had been, he wouldn't have remembered, but he made one up for his friend.

They talked, or rather Dax talked, for almost an hour. He could tell David was tiring, but every time Dax suggested letting David get some rest, his friend would protest, insisting he wanted Dax to stay. The entire time, the dog never left David's side. She, that is—her name was Kobi. David had introduced them — she would readjust her position from time to time, but she wasn't leaving David's side.

Finally, David drifted off to sleep, leaving Dax sitting there.

"He does that," the nurse said, startling Dax. He hadn't heard her come back into the room. "No reflection on the company," she said with a smile. "Mrs. Stephens is waiting for you in the living area."

Dax stood. "Thank you."

As Julia had said, Dax found Marjorie sitting on the living room sofa flipping through a magazine. She dropped it on the table when he walked into the room.

"Sit, please," she said, and Dax took the chair she'd indicated. "How did it go? It's been a while since he's lasted so long with a visitor."

"I think I talked him to sleep," Dax said with a chuckle.

She smiled. "David would like you to stay a couple of days. Will that be an issue?"

Dax thought about Cori. They had a tentative

date for this weekend, but otherwise, his week was fairly open. "No, staying isn't a problem. My days are my own."

"Good. Let me show you where you'll be staying. This part of the house will be left unlocked so you can come in and see David anytime. This way." She gestured toward a pair of French doors. "He's been seeing all his old friends, saying his goodbyes, apologizing to people he hurt. Other than you, he's asked all his friends not to come back after their visit. He said what he wanted to say to them. You're the one he wanted to see last."

Her words hurt him deep in his soul, but also touched his heart.

She led him through a set of French doors to a landscaped pool area, past a row of lounge chairs alongside the pool, to a covered porch that held an outdoor sofa, chairs, and table. Around the corner, and still under the roof, was a fully functional outdoor kitchen. The freestanding structure had been built in the same style and materials as the main house.

"This is our guest house. I think you'll be comfortable here." She opened the glass doors, and Dax walked into another furnished living area with a fireplace and large television. "The bedroom and bath are over there," she said pointing toward the rear of the building. "The kitchen has been stocked, but if there is anything you need or want, please do not hesitate to ask." She picked up a set of keys off the coffee table. "These are the keys to David's truck. Feel free to use it. He sleeps a lot, so don't feel you are confined to our home. This area of Arkansas is beautiful. I hope you'll get out and explore a little. Please make yourself at home."

"That's really nice of you," he said, awed by their generosity.

"Anything for my son." She smiled, but a soulful sadness radiated from her eyes. "I woke you early. I'll let you get some rest."

The next two days, he spent hours sitting with David. Sometimes, they talked. Sometimes, David slept, but Dax stayed close in case his friend woke. Kobi only left David's side for bathroom breaks and the occasional meal, but mostly, the dog remained faithful at his side. It was as if Kobi knew her time with her master was short, and she was going to make the most of it.

He realized early in his stay that he might not make it home for his date. He'd called Marc, who'd promised to contact Cori by Tuesday to let her know that Dax didn't have a phone, but that he'd call when he got back.

As Marjorie had suggested, he did take David's truck for some long drives through the woody mountains. The shiny black truck—a Ford F150—was this year's model, and as far as he could tell, had every option available installed, including custom wheels and chrome accents. The odometer showed less than one thousand miles. David's condition hadn't allowed him much time to enjoy his new truck before he'd become too weak to control the powerful vehicle, or so Marjorie had explained one day.

Monday and Tuesday were the only days Dax felt like David was aware of his presence. Wednesday, as Dax sat at the bedside, David had the first of many seizures. The nurse explained that seizures were expected with glioblastomas as a patient got closer to death.

That evening, Dax was sitting in David's living room with Marjorie and her husband, Harvey, joined him after visiting their son.

"David doesn't have long left," Marjorie said. Her husband put his arm around her as she spoke. "It meant a lot to him, and us, that you spent his last days with him."

"I wish I could have done more," Dax said.

"You did everything you could to expedite his discharge, and we owe you for helping with that," Harvey said.

Dax shook his head. "No, sir. Nothing owed. Nothing due. Anyone in my position would've done the same."

"Maybe, but the fact remains that you were the one who did it," Marjorie said.

Dax glanced at the floor. He'd only done what any human with an ounce of humanity would have done.

"David had asked us to wait until he was gone before we showed you a video he made, but Harvey and I think it's only right you see it now."

Dax frowned. "I don't understand. A video?"

The couple nodded, and Harvey picked up the television remote and pressed some buttons. David's face flashed on the screen.

"He made this video about a week ago," Marjorie explained. "His mind was entirely rational, and we," she took her husband's hand, "are in complete agreement with David's wishes. In fact, we strongly want to fulfill his wishes to the fullest. The video isn't long. Will you watch it?"

Dax nodded. "Okay," he said, but the word was drawn out.

Harvey hit play and David smiled into the camera. "Well, hell, Dax, if you're watching this, I'm dead. But knowing my parents, they're probably showing this to you early." He chuckled. "They're standing against the wall watching me record this," He flashed the camera around and showed both of his parents leaning on the wall. "So, they know exactly what I'm going to say. No surprises for them, just for you. Thank you for giving me the opportunity to see everyone I wanted to say goodbye to. Thank you, also, for all your support and guidance while we were overseas. It was an honor and privilege to serve under you.

"As you have learned by now, I was an only child. What you may not know is that I'm an only child of parents who are only children. That means our family will die out with me." He chuckled and looked toward his parents off screen. "Unless Mom wants to have another baby at fifty."

"Absolutely not," Marjorie said off camera.

David nodded. "I thought not, but I have thought a lot about Kobi." The camera dropped to the Golden Retriever pressed up to him. "She's a great dog, Dax. She was trained for my PTSD." He rubbed the dog's big head. "But when I'm gone, she'll be lost with no job, no one to care for, so, I want you to take her. I know Mom and Dad would keep her, but I think you need her more than they will."

Dax could see tears glistening in David's eyes. "I've never known a better dog. She needs you, Dax, and you need her. Please."

The camera flickered as though there were a break in filming. When David came back on screen, he was more composed.

"I'm leaving you ten million dollars for Kobi's care and upkeep for the rest of her natural life. Feel free to spend the money any way you wish." David held up a hand. "Before you argue, I want you to know why. You are the best man I ever served under. Your men and women didn't follow you because of military hierarchy. They followed your commands because we all knew you would only do what was best for your troops. You are a leader, Dax, and I thank God that you were my leader and my friend. I hope the money will make your life a little better. Thank you, my friend, for being there for me."

The video faded to black. Dax sat frozen on the couch, too stunned to move. "I...I don't understand," he finally choked out.

David's mother joined him on the sofa. "These

are David wishes. We would like you to stay here until he passes. There will be no funeral. He didn't want that." She gave Dax a sad smile. "He said he'd already closed all the doors with past friends and acquaintances and that to hold a public funeral would only reopen those doors. He didn't want that. His request is to be cremated and his ashes scattered in the lake he loved to fish, and that's what we'll do." She lifted a large manilla envelope off the table in front of him. "Here's the transcript of the video for your files. Also, in here is the title of the truck passing from David to you, as well as Kobi's papers."

Dax robotically took the file, still too dumbfounded to fully comprehend the situation. "Thank you," he whispered. "I'm..."

"Shocked, I'm sure," Harvey said. He sat beside his wife. "David respected you like no other man he'd ever met. I hope you will accept these gestures of his, and our, appreciation."

After the Stephens left the room, Dax remained in his near catatonic stupor. He could barely comprehend all the riches David had bestowed. Finally, he stood and went to David's room. His friend was in a late-life coma. Whether he could hear what Dax had to say, Dax didn't know, but he felt like he might.

Dax spent the evening talking to David. Kobi remained by David's side. At some point, Dax's eyes refused to stay open, so he leaned back in the chair for just a second. When he woke, Kobi was sitting by his side, her large head in his lap. As he patted her head, he saw that David was no longer breathing. His parents were on the other side of the bed with tears streaming down their faces.

He stayed until David's ashes were spread, then he loaded up Kobi with all her food and belongings into the truck and headed home. It surprised him that in his mind he'd called Texas home. Maybe it was supposed to be. He'd missed his brother these past years. Moving to Whispering Springs would give him —them—the opportunity to make up for lost time.

The six-hour drive took a little longer since he stopped frequently for Kobi. He didn't know her routine, but was sure they would get used to each other soon enough.

At close to seven on Tuesday evening, he pulled into Marc's house. The lights were on and Marc's car was in the drive. He hadn't told his brother about bringing home a dog...or a truck...or more money than he'd earn in a lifetime.

"Well, Kobi, this is it. Your new home, or at least home for now."

Kobi's head tilted as though comprehending Dax's words.

"My brother Marc lives here. You'll like him." He scratched the dog's chest. "I hope he likes you. Let's go surprise him."

Driving for so long had Dax a little stiff, making his walk more stilted than usual. He'd given up his cane before leaving for Arkansas, and at this moment, he'd love to have something to help support his weight as he walked.

Kobi jumped from the truck and waited as Dax

retrieved Kobi's bed, food, and toys. She'd worn her service vest on the ride down. "Okay, girl. Here we go."

The front door was unlocked, and Dax and Kobi entered.

Marc looked up from the sofa where he sat reading a book. "Welcome back," he said, setting the book on the table beside him. "I'm sorry about your friend."

"Me, too," Dax said "He was a good guy."

Kobi nudged Dax's hand. Reflexively, Dax rubbed her head.

"Who's your new friend?" Marc asked with a tilt of his head toward the golden retriever.

"This is Kobi. She's, um, going to be living with me."

Marc arched an eyebrow. "Is that so?"

Dax stiffened his back. "Yes, that's so. She belonged to David, and he asked me to give her a good home. So, that's what I plan to do. If you need me to move out because of her, I will," he said in a rigid, determined voice.

Marc held up his hand. "I didn't say anything like that, so chill out. I see her vest. What is she trained for?"

"David had PTSD. Kobi helped him cope with it. His parents said that David would have nightmares often, and Kobi would wake him up."

Marc eyed Dax. "That's interesting."

"Are you implying I need a PTSD dog?"

"Nope, man. I'm not. I'm just saying she might be helpful if you have one of your nightmares."

Dax snorted. "I don't have nightmares."

Marc didn't reply.

"You did tell Cori where I was, right?" Dax asked, mostly to change the subject. He knew he could trust his brother.

"Yeah, I called her, but, um, it wasn't on Monday."

"That's okay," Dax assured him. "Letting her know on Tuesday was fine. I'd have felt bad if I'd left her hanging all week."

Marc's gaze flashed away from Dax and onto the wall.

Dax narrowed his eyes. "Marc, what did you do?"

"Well, you see, it was a busy week, and I forgot to call Cori until Friday." At least his brother had the courtesy to look embarrassed.

Dax groaned.

"I'm sorry, man," Marc said. "That rustling ring hit again last week, and I was slammed from morning to night."

Dax turned toward the door.

"Where're you going?" Marc asked.

"To Cori's house. I think I owe her an apology. Plus, I want to introduce her to Kobi."

Back in the car, he made a quick stop to pick up fresh flowers. Women always enjoyed getting flowers...he hoped.

Nine

Cori slipped the gold hoop earrings into her ear lobes. Getting ice cream with Greg on Sunday night had been a mistake. Agreeing to have dinner tonight was a bigger one. She'd loved him once. She'd planned on spending the rest of her life with him, until he'd told her he wasn't ready for marriage and walked away. When she'd heard he'd married someone else only six months later, she'd been wounded in the worst way. Not only had his marriage been a blow to her heart, it had been a solid punch to her ego. All her childhood insecurities had come rushing back with a vengeance. Thank goodness she'd found a skilled therapist who'd helped her put her life back together.

Still, seeing him again, his being so attentive and kind, had rattled her. She wasn't in love with him any longer, and she didn't want to love him again. She'd realized that no matter her draw to his physical attributes—and he remained as handsome and fit as the day they'd met—she couldn't trust him. Words were easy to say. Actions to convey feelings were much harder.

Take Dax, for example. The night under the stars, watching a meteor shower, had been his way of showing her he had listened and he was sorry for his actions. She couldn't blame him for his lack of response last week when he'd believed she was aware of his trip. From what Marc had said, the trip had been unexpected, and Dax had had to leave quickly, so forgetting his cell phone was understandable.

She slipped her feet into her heels. Tonight, she'd explain to Greg that their past was exactly that, the past. If his primary reason for moving to Whispering Springs was to reignite their relationship, it was pointless. She had no desire to go back.

When her doorbell rang, she checked the clock beside her bed. Greg was twenty minutes early. Maybe she should tell him everything before they left the house. He might want to not get dinner.

"Coming," she called as she hurried toward the door.

She flung the door open, fully expecting to see her date. Instead, Dax wrapped his arms around her waist and pulled her against his chest. His mouth found hers with a moan. He licked along the seam of her lips, and she opened her mouth. He thrust his tongue into her mouth, stroking and touching all the areas inside.

She snaked her arms around his neck and held him tight. At the sight of him, her heart had shot off like a rocket, blasting the rate way too high. Her stomach clenched as a wave of euphoria swept over her. Her tongue dueled with his before she pulled it into her mouth to taste him. God, she'd missed him.

With his arms around her waist, he lifted her off the floor and walked into her house, slamming the door with foot. They continued to kiss, drinking from each other's mouths like they were parched.

Finally, Dax pulled back and kissed her forehead. "I missed you."

The smile that formed on her lips was full of joy and happiness. "I missed you too."

He put his forehead against hers. "I'm so sorry Marc didn't let you know where I was until Friday. I didn't have your phone number to call you myself, but I knew once he explained, you'd understand why I left so abruptly."

"I'm sorry about your friend," she said as she rubbed her hands up and down his back. "That must have been hard."

His eyes shut, and he drew in a breath. "It was. David was a great guy. I hadn't met his parents until this past week, but I can see where he got his character. I really liked Marjorie and Harvey." He kissed her again, as if he couldn't get enough.

She liked his hunger for her, his obvious desire, if the cock straining his jeans was an indication of his interest.

"I have someone I want you to meet." He stepped back and stopped. Confusion flashed on his face. "Why are you dressed up? Were you headed out?"

"Um, yeah," she said, heat rushing up her neck. "An old friend is in town and we're having dinner." That wasn't a total lie. Greg was an old friend, and they were only having dinner.

The bell rang, followed by a knocking on her door.

Her ex's timing couldn't be worse. First, he'd shown back up in her life right as she'd met someone new, whom she really liked. And second, he arrived ten minutes early for their date before she could explain everything to Dax.

"Your friend seems a little anxious to get going," Dax said, with a warm smile. "I'm sorry I dropped in without warning."

She took his hand and brought his knuckles to her lips. "I'm glad you came. I'm sorry I have plans. If I'd known..." She frowned. "Who did you want me to meet?"

The doorbell rang again.

She sighed. "I'm sorry. I'm going to have to get that."

He chuckled. "You girls don't get into too much trouble tonight."

"Um..." She walked toward the door and said over her shoulder, "My friend isn't a girl."

"Hi, honey," Greg said when she opened the door. "You ready to go?"

Cori stepped back when Greg reached for her. "In a minute," she said, glancing over her shoulder at Dax. "I have company."

Greg stepped into her living room and eyed Dax.

"I'm Greg Simmons, Ree's fiancé," he said, extending his hand to Dax. "You must be one of Ree's patients."

Cori's eyes opened wide and flashed to Dax. "No, Greg. Dax is a good friend, not a patient, and you are *not* my fiancé," she said emphatically.

He gave a casual shrug and winked at her. "That's only a matter of time." To Dax he said, "Ree is the love of my life. I've come home to marry her."

Dax stood frozen in place, his face a mask of confusion.

"Greg, stop it," Cori said firmly. "We're not getting married. In fact, we're not even going to dinner tonight. I was planning to telling you this later tonight, but we aren't getting back together. I've moved on. I moved on ten years ago when you left. I have no intention of going backwards. I'd hope we could be friendly, if not friends, but I can see I was mistaken."

Greg stepped toward Cori with his hands outstretched. "I'm sorry, honey, don't be that way." He took her hands. "Let's talk about this over dinner. We have reservations at the Mansion at Turtle Creek. Let's start again and have a nice evening."

She jerked her hands back. "Greg, honestly, I think it would be better if we didn't go to dinner and you left."

"Now, Ree, I know how you get when it's your time of the month." He looked at Dax with a grin. "You know what I mean, right, man?"

Dax's head jerked back and his gaze found Cori. "Would you like me to get rid of him?"

Cori chuckled. "He's just leaving, right, Greg? You're leaving before this ex-Army Delta Force Major kicks your ass."

Greg sucked in a breath. "We're not done, Ree. Not by a long shot." He marched to the door and turned back. "You have my phone number. I'll be expecting an apology call by tomorrow." He slammed the door behind him.

Cori's living room went deathly silent before she heard Dax begin to chortle. Then she snickered, followed by Dax's deep laugh. She snorted and then a laugh rose from deep inside her. Clutching her waist, she doubled over with laughter.

"Holy hell," Dax said. "What was that?"

Tears were rolling down Cori's face as she looked at him.

His expression grew serious. "Are you okay?" He rushed over to her. "Cori?"

Wiping her tears, she said, "I'm fine. Good lord, once upon a time, I almost married that man." She cleared her throat. "I think I dodged a bullet." As the common phrase left her mouth, she realized what she'd said and to whom. Her eyes grew wide, and she slapped her hand over her mouth. "Ohmigod, Dax. I'm sorry. That was so rude of me."

He wrapped his arms around her. "Hey, no biggie. I'm glad you dodged that bullet." He hugged her, then lifted her chin until their mouths met in a long kiss.

When the kiss finally ended, she sighed and leaned her head on his chest. His heart beat rapidly under her ear. She smiled, knowing he was as affected by their kiss as she was.

"Have you had dinner?" she asked. "I'm all dressed up with nowhere to go."

He chuckled. "I could eat."

With a laugh, she bumped her shoulder against his chest. "What sounds good?"

"Oh! I totally forgot. There's someone in the truck you should meet."

"Oh God, it's not an ex-fiancée, is it? I don't think I can take another blast from the past."

With a laugh, he pulled her to him. "No, but she is a new girl in my life. Her name is Kobi, and I think you'll love her. Come on. We'll find someplace that'll take all of us."

Cori was a little skeptical of meeting this new girl in Dax's life, especially one with such beautiful gold hair. But her four legs and doggy breath won Cori over in a heartbeat.

They ended up at Leo's Bar and Grill, a local joint known for cold beer and thick, juicy hamburgers. With Kobi's service vest, Cori knew they could have gone anywhere, but Leo's new deck was ideal for a May evening.

"She's beautiful," Cori said, scratching Kobi's head.

"I think so too. I haven't had a dog since I was a kid. I have a lot to remember."

"You said you'd tell me about last week over dinner and how Kobi came to be yours."

Dax sighed. "Well, I got a call very early last Monday..."

Over a dinner of cheeseburgers, Dax told Cori about the week, Kobi, and the truck he'd inherited.

Cori's heart ached for the obvious pain she heard in Dax's words. Last week had been hard on him. Another one of his men gone. She recognized his survivor's guilt, but wondered if he did, not that she had any intention of telling him. Gifting Dax a PTSD trained dog was interesting, however. He'd never told her about any nightmares he'd had or trouble sleeping, but with all the trauma he'd endured, all the men he'd lost to war, and now to cancer—all things outside his control—any person with an ounce of humanity would be affected.

"Wow, Dax. That's a lot to process. You doing okay?"

"Yeah, I'm fine." He frowned. "My only confusion is Kobi. I mean, David's parents were great, and I know she would have had a wonderful life with them. I'm not sure why David was so insistent that I take Kobi."

"David sounds like he was a smart guy," she said. "Sounds like he knew you'd give her a good home."

Dax leaned over to rub Kobi's head. "I will."

The love and caring in Dax's eyes for Kobi touched Cori's heart. Dax had so much love to give, and so much life left to live. She hoped he could learn to accept and appreciate that.

"So, tell me about this Greg guy," Dax said. "You must have loved him if you were going to marry him."

She sighed and leaned back in her chair. "I did love him, as much as someone at that age can. Sometimes looking back, I wonder if I was in love with being in love, or was I in love with Greg."

"And?"

With a shrug, she said, "I'm not sure."

"His coming back into your life must've been a surprise."

"Huge."

"I didn't mean to interrupt your plans tonight."

She smiled. "I'm okay with it."

He rubbed Kobi's back. "Maybe you should have gone out with him tonight."

Her heart sank at his words. "What...What are you talking about?"

"You need to be sure."

She frowned. "Sure of what?"

His gaze studied her face. "You need to be sure that he isn't the one for you."

"Dax." She leaned over and took his hand. "He's not the one for me."

"I need you to know that beyond any doubts." He laced his fingers with hers. "I don't want to start something with you if there are lingering doubts. I've had enough loss to last me a lifetime." He squeezed her fingers. "I like you, Cori. I like you a lot."

"I like you a lot, Dax."

He smiled, but nerves showed on his face. "I'd

like to give this a shot...us, I mean, but I don't want to start anything if you still have feelings for Greg, and I understand if you do. I believe love is forever."

"I do too—and that's why I wonder if I was really in love with him or in love with the idea of being in love."

"At the time, though, you believed you were in love with Greg. Why did you end the engagement? Were you having doubts about him?" He sighed. "I'm sorry for asking all these questions about your past, but I need to understand."

He's protecting his heart, she thought. She could understand that. Hadn't he experienced enough disappointments in his life? He was hesitant to start something that could hurt him. She understood.

"Ugh, here's what happened." She shook her head and drew in a deep breath to continue. "I hate to even relive those memories, but here goes. He and I were living together. I'd just finished my written comprehensive exams for my master's degree and hurried home to share my excitement." She smiled. "I kicked some serious ass on those tests."

"I bet you did."

"I did. I thought maybe we could go out to celebrate or something. When I got home, my sister was at the apartment with him?"

"Your sister?"

"Yeah, Elsie Belle. They were sitting on the sofa, their heads together as they spoke quietly in low whispers. Elsie stood and said, 'I've got to go. Good to see you. How were the finals?' and left without my ever saying a word. She hustled out of our apartment so fast I didn't have time to say hello or goodbye. Greg had a sheepish expression on his face, and it made me wonder about their conversation. I didn't have to wait long to discover what they'd been talking about.

"That evening, we went out to celebrate, but he was subdued the whole night. The next day I had some errands to run. When I got home, his luggage was sitting by the door. I said, 'Greg, what going on?'" He said, 'We need to talk.'" She gave a slight shoulder shrug. "No good conversation starts with those words, am I right?"

Dax scoffed.

"We sat down on the sofa and he said, 'You're a special person,' which made me groan. Another sentence that nothing good can follow, right?"

Dax nodded. "Go on." He held up one finger. "But first I want to say, he was right about that. You are a special person."

His words filled her soul with happiness. "Thank you. Anyway, he said that he didn't want to hurt me, but that he didn't think he was ready for marriage. I was fine with that. I'd been accepted into a doctoral program, and I knew I was going to be busy for the next few years. I was good with waiting. But then he said that wasn't what he meant. Time wasn't his issue. He wanted to break up so he could date around more. I was stunned. I mean, we'd been together for four years. We weren't children." She waved her hand. "Anyway, long story short, we broke up, he insisted on getting his ring back, and he left. Six months later, he married someone else."

"Ouch," Dax said.

"Exactly. I went on with my life and before I knew it, ten years had passed. Then Saturday he showed up in my driveaway wanting a second chance."

"He smarted up and realized what he'd given up," Dax said.

"We had ice cream sundaes on Sunday, and he told me that my sister had put doubts in his head. That day I found her at the apartment, she'd pointed out how young we were and how we had our whole lives ahead of us, and was he really sure marriage to me was what he really wanted. He said he'd already had some reservations and that conversation tipped the scales, so he left." She looked at Dax. "And that was the last time I spoke to him until last Saturday when he showed up in my front yard."

"He broke up with you?" Dax said, his voice tinged with incongruity. "Was he insane?"

She laughed. "No, well, maybe. I think the part that hurt worse was his getting married so quickly after we split."

"But that doesn't explain why he married someone else."

"And had children with her," she said. "One or two, I don't really remember. I kind of lost track."

"Wow. So, he's divorced."

"I guess so. I didn't ask."

Dax's hand that'd been stroking Kobi stilled. "I

can't believe someone could be so blind as to break up with you and leave."

She smiled, as did her heart. "Thank you. That's so sweet."

"No, not sweet. Honest."

"Yeah, you're being sweet, and that's okay. I can take it." And she could. She'd told her story, she'd waited for the tears to form, or the nausea to develop in her stomach, or that overwhelming feeling of despair, but none of those things happened. It was a story, almost like it was someone else and not her.

"I'm confused then," he said. "I'm not sure I understand why you made plans to go with dinner with him tonight."

"Why did I make plans to go out with him? Well, that's a good question, and I'm embarrassed to answer."

"Why are you embarrassed?"

"I'm not sure you're going to understand."

Dax pulled his hand back and leaned against his chair. "Try me."

"He walked away from me. I always swore if he came back, I'd make him crawl. I know as a psychologist that's not a healthy reaction, but he came back begging and pleading for another chance."

"You wanted to give him that chance?"

"No, that's not it at all. I think his begging for a second chance was good for my ego more than my having a sincere interest in being with him again." Heat flushed on her face.

"So," he said with a sigh, "where do you stand with him?"

She laughed. "I'm certainly not going to call with an apology in the morning."

"Good."

"But here's the thing, Dax. I need to see him. I need to tell him we—him and me—have no future, and I need to tell him that face-to-face, not by text or email, or even a phone call."

He nodded. "Okay, so you are going to see him again."

"One time," she said. "Just to make sure he understands we are over and nothing he says or does will change that."

"Okay," he said, "and when you've done that, and you know...when you know beyond a shadow of a doubt that you've left him and that relationship in past, call me, and I'll be here."

Ten

The drive from the restaurant back to Cori's house was quiet. For Dax, their conversation had been emotionally draining. He was out of words. Was Cori feeling the same? No words left?

He pulled to a stop in front of her house.

"Thank you for dinner," she said, her tone more formal than usual.

"Cori." He reached over and took her hand. "Call me when you know what you want. I'll understand if you pick Greg." He forced a smile he hoped was friendlier than he felt. "I'll be disappointed, but I'm used to that."

She glanced down at their hands and back to him. "I'll call you."

He leaned over and kissed her gently. "I'll hope you do."

He and Kobi watched her walk away and into her house. "Well, girl, we've laid it on the line."

Kobi barked.

"I know. I like her too."

An unfamiliar truck was parked in the drive of Marc's house when he got back. It didn't look new, but the truck was definitely a late model. To his surprise, Sami was sitting on the sofa with Marc when he walked in.

"Oh, who's this?" Sami said, reaching her hand out and then pulling it back. "Sorry. I just saw the vest. When did you get a service dog?"

"A gift from my friend who died last week. As long as she's wearing the vest, she knows she's on the job. Hold on." He unclipped the vest and slipped it over Kobi's head. The effect was as if he'd released her from her job. Her entire demeanor changed from professional working dog to house pet. Her butt began to wiggle as her swinging tail cleared papers and magazines off the coffee table. "Her name is Kobi."

"Kobi," Sami cooed. "Come here, baby."

Kobi landed on the sofa with all four paws. She settled on the cushion between Sami and Marc.

"You were gone longer than I expected," Marc said.

"We grabbed dinner."

"Are you dating someone?" Sami asked. "Already? You haven't been here that long. Who?"

Dax had no intention of going into details with his nosey sister. "Nobody you know, and not really dating."

Marc's eyebrow arched, but Dax ignored him.

"Besides, I want to hear about your job search,"

Dax said, changing the subject. "Which offer did you accept?"

Sami's face brightened with a beaming smile. "Whispering Springs Police Department. I'm so excited."

"Why that instead of your other option with the county sheriff in Diamond Lakes?" Dax asked.

"Better pay, mostly. I liked Chief Gruber, but I also liked Sheriff Monroe. Gruber seems...I don't know... like he'd take less bullshit. I think my military experience fits his style better."

"I assume you have to go to a police academy first."

She nodded. "I have to attend the police academy in Dallas. The program is twenty-two weeks, so it'll be close to six months before I start here."

"What's the plan?" Dax asked.

"Funny you should ask that. Marc and I were just talking about that. It makes no sense for me to drive to and from school every day from here. That's a lot of lost time. So, I thought I'd find a short-term rental and live near the school. When I'm done, I'll find something here."

"That's fine," Marc said, "but you have to be the one to tell Mom. I doubt she's going to be thrilled with the news."

Sami shrugged her shoulders and then draped her body over Kobi. "I'm an adult. Mom will just have to accept that I want to live close to both my brothers."

"Dax never said he was going to live here," Marc pointed out.

She just smiled at her older brother. "Didn't say he wasn't either." Standing, she stretched her arms over her head. "I'm headed to bed. See you guys in the A.M."

Marc started to rise, probably to head to bed also, but Dax waved him back down. "Hang on," he said. "I want to talk to you about something."

Marc sat. "Okay. What's up?"

Dax hadn't told anyone about the money David had left for him, and he wasn't ready to talk about it yet.

"The Hanson Ranch. Did you make a decision?"

Marc dragged his fingers through his hair. "I want it. I just can't figure out how to pay for it. You asked me about a loan, and a bank would loan on that property. The problem is there is no way I could make the payments."

"You never told me what the Hanson family offered it to you for."

Marc sighed. "One million dollars. Half or less of what they'll get for it on the open market, but that's what their parents wanted them to do, so they made me the offer."

"You have to take it," Dax said. "You'd be crazy not to. Is there a real estate agent involved?"

Marc nodded. "I'm excluded from their contact, meaning if I buy it, the agent—her name if Hillary Hillerman—will get one-percent of the sale price."

"It's listed then?"

"Yes."

"I'd like to buy the property with you."

Marc's eyes popped open wide. "Are you serious?"

"I am. It's a good investment. I've loved what I've seen of it. It would be great to do this with you, but the question is, do you want a partner?"

"Anyone else, I'd say no, but you? Hell, yeah."

Dax released his breath. "Good."

Marc chuckled. "Did you think I'd say no?"

Dax shrugged. "I wasn't sure how you'd feel about sharing your ranch dream with someone else."

"That's the thing, Dax. You're not *someone else*. You're my brother, and I can't think of anything I'd like more. You're okay with the asking price?"

"If you're asking if I've got the five-hundred-thousand for my half, yeah. That's not a problem."

Marc arched an eyebrow. "Military paid way better than I thought."

Dax grinned. "It's a long story, and I'll tell you the long tale one day, but for tonight, give me the agent's phone number, and I can get the ball rolling while you're at work tomorrow."

Marc stood. "Perfect. Thanks, partner." He held out his hand, and Dax shook it.

"Partners."

"Now, the hard question," Marc said. "Why? Why would you sink so much money into a place you've never lived? Does this have anything to do with Cori Lambert?"

Dax scratched the itch on his neck and, with a wince, said, "I don't know. Maybe? But regardless of what happens there, I've missed my family. I want to live with my family."

"And Maine is totally out of the question?" Before Dax could reply, Marc said, "Never mind. Mom would drive you off a rocky cliff up there. She'd love you to death."

"Exactly. I love Mom and Dad, but..."

"Say no more, partner. Welcome to Texas."

Bullets flew around him. Men's screams ripped through his soul. Blood. So much blood everywhere. Explosions filled the air with smoke and debris.

"Take cover. Take cover," Dax called out to his men.

"Incoming," his second-in-command yelled.

Dax hit the ground. An explosion behind him sent shards of glass into his back. His body jerked as bullets peppered his legs.

"Help me," he called out. "Medic. I need a medic."

Then something cold pressed against his cheek, followed by bright light. A warm, weight settled over his body.

Dax's eyes flew open. The lights were on in his room. Kobi was stretched across his chest, her breath blowing in his face.

He blew out a long breath. "Thanks, girl." He stroked his hand down her back. "That was a bad one," he confessed.

Kobi nuzzled against his neck. Dax felt his tense muscles begin to loosen, and he relaxed into his mattress. He continued running his palm through Kobi's soft fur until he felt his eyelids grow heavy.

The next thing he knew, sunlight poured through his window. Kobi was tucked tight against his side. He felt...rested, something he'd not experienced in a very long time.

As if sensing he was awake, Kobi's head popped up off the mattress. She pressed her nose to his cheek.

"Good morning to you." He patted the top of her head. "Sorry about last night, but I appreciated your help."

The dog panted, and if anyone had asked, Dax would have sworn she smiled.

"How about some breakfast?"

Those were the magic words. Kobi jumped off the bed and waited by Dax's closed door.

He chuckled. Dog ownership agreed with him.

Dax was the only one in the kitchen. Both Sami and Marc had already left. The note on the table from Sami said she loved him and she'd see him in a week or so. She'd added that Marc had left before she had, saying something about cattle rustling.

He had no trouble finding the Whispering Springs Realty office in the downtown square. This morning, the town square was alive with people going in and out of shops, and cars circling as their drivers looked for parking places. Dax lucked into a parking park only a few doors down from the real estate office. He and Kobi hopped out and headed for the entrance of the real estate office. The office was small, with a reception desk right inside the front door.

"Good morning," an older woman said from behind the receptionist's desk. "Can I help you?"

"Good morning. I'm looking for Hillary Hillerman."

The woman's face broke into a bright smile. "That's me. I'm manning the receptionist desk as our usual receptionist is out on maternity leave." She stood and extended her hand.

Dax shook her hand and said, "I'm Dax Cooper."

That's all he got out before she said, "Oh, yes, Mr. Cooper. You're Sheriff Singer's brother, isn't that right?"

Dax tilted his head and chuckled. "That's true."

She grinned. "Our gossip mill is usually fairly accurate. What can I do for you, Mr. Cooper? Looking for property in our area?"

"It's Dax, and yes. Specifically, the Hanson Ranch. I understand from my brother that he and the family have settled on a price for that property. We—he and I—are going to buy the land. I'd like you to draw up a contract for the sale."

Her eyes opened in surprise. "Well...that's great. I'll get another agent to take my place up here, and we can go to my office."

In her office, which he noted was large and plush with a highly polished desk, displaying a name plate and computer, she wasted no time with pleasantries and immediately got to work.

"Now, are we talking about a joint ownership situation?"

Dax nodded. "That's correct."

She nodded and typed something into her computer. "Now, let's talk loans. Have you been preapproved, or will the contract be contingent on being able to secure financing?"

"No financing. I'll be paying cash."

Her gaze jerked from the monitor to his face. "Cash? A million in cash?"

"That's correct. I have the funds ready to transfer at closing, which we'd like as soon as possible."

"Is your brother aware of this?"

Dax shook his head. "No, it's a birthday present surprise." He smiled. "I hope you can keep a secret."

"I can, but he will have to sign this offer too."

"I'm sure you can figure out a way to get his signature on that offer without telling I'll be paying cash." He lifted an eyebrow. "That isn't a problem, is it? I'd hate to ruin his birthday surprise."

She waved him off. "I'll get it done, Mr. Cooper. Now, do you want to leave some earnest money?"

"I can, if I need to, but I believe the Hanson family knows we're serious about this purchase without it. My bank is out of state, but I'll be setting up a local account today. I can drop off a check later, or give you one now. Never mind. I'll write a check." He pulled out his wallet and removed the check he kept with him in case of need. Today was as big of a need as he'd had in a while. He filled out the check except for the payee. "Who do I make this check out to?"

"Whispering Springs Realty will be fine."

He completed the check and signed it. "Here you go."

She took the check, her eyes registering surprise. "One-hundred-thousand in earnest money will definitely get the family onboard with the sale. Thank you."

"Remember, my brother's name will be on the deed with mine, but I want the full payment aspect to be a surprise."

"I understand. This will certainly be a memorable birthday for Sheriff Singer."

Dax smiled. "That's the idea. Oh, and one more thing. I need the name of a good general contractor."

"I've got three names I can give you."

"Perfect."

In his truck, he called Marc. "Hey, I need a bank in this area."

His brother chuckled. "Well, good morning to you too."

"Sorry," Dax said with a snort. "My mind is racing with a list of things I want to get done today."

"I use Texas Bank of Whispering Springs."

"Thanks. Talk to you later."

He finished his errands, disappointed not to hear from Cori. Had he drawn the line in the sand too deep?

Marc called in the middle of the afternoon. "What are you doing?"

"Nothing. What's up?'

"I'll run by and pick you up. Let's take a drive."

Shortly afterward, a white SUV with SHERIFF stenciled across the side pulled up. Dax and Kobi met Marc in the drive and climbed in.

"Where are we headed?" Dax asked.

Marc's grin was huge. His eyes sparked as he said, "To see our ranch."

Dax slapped his brother's shoulder. "Done deal, then?"

"Will be. Hillary dropped by the station and got my signature on the order. Since I had a basic oral agreement with the family, this should slip through like a greased pig."

Dax could feel the excitement vibrating off his brother. Man, he loved being able to do something like this for his family. When Sami finished the police academy and moved back to Whispering Springs, he might try to surprise her with a house. He made a mental note to talk to Hillary about it. If he got Hillary to work with Sami, he'd know which house to buy.

When he'd gone into the military, he'd pretty much accepted he'd never live to an old age. However, now that it appeared he would live past fifty, and David Stephens had given him more money than he could spend in three lifetimes, whatever he could do for his family would be high on his list.

As far as Dax was concerned, he had his family, and that was probably all he could ask for. With his missing leg, and multiple scars, finding love and starting his own family was a pipedream. He'd thought Cori could look past his faults, but her going out with an old boyfriend who'd retained his good looks the minute Dax had been out of town had made him wonder if Cori felt sorrier for him than attracted to him.

"Where'd you go?" Marc asked. "I've been talking to you for the last ten minutes."

Dax chuckled. "Just thinking." He pointed to an area beyond the fence as they neared the Hanson ranch. "I was thinking about building there."

"You can, but I have a better place in mind." Marc pulled into the drive, unlocked the gate, and drove on. "As soon as I can afford it, I want to put in an electric gate. This locking and unlocking is a pain."

Dax nodded. "Okay." He added that to his to-do list.

"I really want to renovate the main house for me to live in," Marc said. "Is that a problem for you?"

Dax laughed. "Absolutely not. I want something new, new, new. By the way, do you have someone in mind to do the work?"

"Yeah. Cash Montgomery."

"And he's our...?"

"First cousin. Youngest son of Lane. Used to be a bull rider. Got hurt. Damned near died. Didn't take to cowboying when he got home. He renovated Caroline Graham Montgomery's grandfather's house and got bit by the construction bug. He still works as a part-time deputy when I need help."

Dax frowned. "Caroline, as in Travis's wife had family in the area?"

Marc chuckled. "That's a long story for another time. I've got something I want to show you."

Marc drove past the house and followed a rutted, barely-there road until it ended at a large pond. "I thought you might want to build back here. The pond is five acres, so fishing would be good. It's quiet and private, but not so far away from the main areas of the ranch. What do you think? You could fence in a yard area and keep out whatever livestock we have."

Dax looked around, and it was what he'd suspected. This was the spot he'd brought Cori on their second date. He wondered if his brother knew this location would hold special memories. "It's a good plan, but we have lots of time for that. Building a house is a long project. Let's get you in first and then work on a place for me."

While Dax thought he'd probably stay in Whispering Springs, once he got his brother and sister settled, he could still move on if he wanted. This town was small. Gossip flowed freely. He might be better served moving where he could retain some anonymity. Besides, if Cori and Greg got back together, he'd see her everywhere, and he didn't want that.

All the way home, Marc talked nonstop about his plans for the ranch. His enthusiasm made Dax happy, even if he personally didn't feel the excitement.

As he lay down for the night, a heavy weariness

draped over him. Cori hadn't called that day. She didn't call the next either.

The week passed without hearing from Cori. Either she was very busy or she'd made her decision, and it wasn't him.

Eleven

⤛⟋⟍⤜

The dinner with Dax had left Cori edgy. She wasn't happy with how they'd left things, especially his putting the decision regarding continuing their relationship on her. She'd come home emotionally drained, sure that she didn't want Greg back in her life. And yes, she realized she was being petty that she enjoyed having the power to send him away this time instead of him leaving her.

Every day, a floral arrangement from Greg had arrived at her office. Such a predictable reaction from him. Her office and receptionist area were beginning to take on the floral scents of a funeral home. She had to deal with Greg, but she kept putting it off. What was stopping her from calling him up and telling him she'd moved on? She had moved on, right? The only person she'd relied on for advice was a professor from her training program.

During her doctoral program, Cori had gotten

close to Dr. Rosemary Ross, her clinical professor. They still spoke once or twice a month, but mostly it was on an informal, friendly basis. However, whenever Cori needed a professional ear to listen, or a professional opinion on a case, her first call was always to Rosemary Ross.

Friday morning, on the drive to her office, Cori decided she needed a good listener, so once she settled behind her desk with a cup of coffee, she placed the call.

"Good morning. Rosemary Ross's office. How may I help you?"

"Good morning. This is Dr. Cora Lambert. Is Rosemary available to take a call?"

"Let me check."

A few seconds later, there was a click, and Cori heard, "Cora Belle Lambert. It's about time you called me."

Cori chuckled. "How's New York?"

Dr. Ross had taken a new position at Columbia University which was keeping her busy and challenged.

"It's not Texas."

This time Cori laughed. "No cowboys? No horses?"

"Oh, there are horses, but riding them are city cops, not cowboys."

"Ah," Cori said. "Totally different."

"You got that right. Now, it's early for you down there in Texas. Got a troublesome patient?"

"Yes and no. A troublesome issue, yes, but it's not a patient. It's me."

"Oh?"

Cori heard her old friend take a sip of coffee.

"Lucky for you," Rosemary said, "the student who was coming for counseling this morning canceled, so I'm all yours. What's happening?"

"You remember my fiancé, Greg Simmons?"

"Of course, I do. The one who walked out on you, broke your heart, and left your crushed? I have a vague memory of him. Why?"

"He dropped in last Saturday. At my house."

"With wife and children?" Rosemary's voice was sharp with sarcasm.

"No. Said he'd left them. Said he made a mistake when he left me, and he still loves me. Said he wants us to get back together, and that he wants to marry me."

"I see."

In her mind's eye, Cori could see her friend sitting back in her chair, her fingers templed in front of her.

"And how do you feel about this?"

Cori grinned, even though only she knew that. "Conflicted," she confessed.

"Why? Are you still in love with him? Are you worried about hurting his ex-wife and family?"

It hit Cori that she hadn't given much, if any, thought to the hurt and pain his family had to be experiencing with Greg's betrayal. Ouch. Guilt punched her in the gut.

"Wow, Rosemary. You didn't pull your punches with these questions."

"I rarely do. So, talk to me. What's going on inside your head?"

"I met this new guy recently. I like him, but it's early."

"Oh, goody. I love a story that begins 'once upon a time, I met a guy.'"

Cori chuckled. "His name is Dax. He's new in town. We've been out a few times."

"Sounds promising, and...?"

"He's had a rough time of it. He's ex-military. Got badly hurt in the final days of the war in Afghanistan."

"I'm sorry to hear that. How's he doing now?"

"Physically, okay. Some burn scars that bother him more than the people around him."

"Unfortunately, people can be judgmental about non-perfection."

Cori sighed. "He's also missing part of his left leg, not that I've actually seen his prosthesis. He keeps it hidden under jeans all the time. On his inside, he's so beautiful, and I don't think he knows it."

"I remember Greg as being quite handsome and flirty, and he knew it. In fact, after you and Greg split up, it seemed like most of the men I saw you with were pretty boys. Are you saying Dax isn't handsome?"

"No, I'm not saying that at all. He's very attractive. I don't think he even realizes how good-looking he actually is. Sure, he has some scars, but they don't distract from the man he is, and I don't think he can see that. His soul shines through his eyes."

"He sounds like quite a guy. Did you call to talk about him, or did you call to talk about Greg?"

Cori leaned back in her chair. "Well...that's the issue..."

"What's the issue? Are you comparing the two of them? Trying to decide between them?"

"Comparing them? I wasn't, but now you've got me doing just that. Dax isn't perfect on the outside, but he's perfect on the inside. He's perfect for me. Whereas Greg's exterior is handsome, but his soul? How could he leave his wife and children for an old girlfriend, especially one he hasn't spoken to in nearly ten years."

"Good point. A decade with no contact and he expects you to drop everything for him?"

"When you put it like that, it's kind of crazy," Cori said.

Rosemary cleared her throat. "Could it be that he runs from his problems? Is it possible that his marriage is having trouble, and his response is to run away? Isn't that exactly what he did with you? Didn't he decide he wasn't ready to marry, and rather than work through whatever issue he had, he simply walked away? Maybe running away is his answer to any difficult situation."

"Good observation. It's interesting how it's so clear when you point it out, but I'm still not sure what he's trying to prove."

"Let me see if I've got the picture. You're dating

Dax, and you like him. But then your old fiancé shows up on your doorstep, and what happens? You faint? You toss him out on his ear? You fall to the ground to welcome him back?"

"Nothing so dramatic, I'm afraid. Actually, I felt nothing. We had ice cream and talked, but it wasn't like it'd been back in the day. No sweaty palms. No racing heart. No head swimming in lust. No butterflies. Just a good-looking man sitting across the table."

"Interesting," Rosemary said. "What happens when you're around Dax?"

Cori smiled and sighed wistfully. "Sweaty palms. Racing heart. Butterflies by the millions in my stomach."

"I'm confused as to what your problem is. Send Greg back to his wife and carry on—and I mean that literally—with Dax."

"That's what I should do, but..."

"But you haven't sent Greg away."

"Correct."

"Why not?"

Cori shut her eyes as if to shut out the harsh truth. "You are going to think me horrible, petty even, but I want to hurt Greg emotionally. I want him to feel the pain I felt when he left me. That's awful, right?"

Her friend chuckled. "It's human, my dear."

"I know." Cori sighed. "Dax and I had a little tiff over Greg."

"Tell me what happened."

"On Tuesday, Dax came by my house. He'd been out of town for a week, so his dropping by was a surprise. A good one," she hurriedly added. "But I had dinner plans with Greg that night. I'd planned to tell him I wasn't going back to him. Greg arrived while Dax was still in my living room. There were words exchanged, and Greg left in a huff."

"Let me guess. Dax said, or at least implied, *me or him*? Pick one. Am I right?"

"Yes," she replied with another long sigh.

"And now, the time has come that you have to act."

"Correct."

"I'm sorry, Cora, but time is not your friend here. You're not being fair to either man. You're giving false hope to Greg while keeping Dax on the back burner."

"I'll be honest…"

"Yes, it's about time you were." Rosemary's words were firm but her tone was gentle.

"I don't want to see Greg."

"You don't have to see him. You're not required to have a meal with him before brushing him off. You can send him a text. Send a telegram. You can call him. You can sky write it. *No, Greg. Not interested.* That's all you have to say."

"I don't think he'll stop so easily. He's sent flowers every day. I don't think a simple 'no' will be enough."

Her friend chuckled. "Sounds like your Dax

could deliver that message in a method he would understand."

Cori laughed. "Probably. But I promised Dax I wouldn't reach out to him until I was done with Greg."

"Fine. Send Greg a text as soon as we hang up and tell him you've thought about it, and thank you for the flowers, but no, I've moved on. I'm happy with my life, and don't want you back in it. That's it. That's all you have to say, and then block his number. You don't have to see him to say that."

"But I'm an adult. Shouldn't I do better?"

"So what? You're an adult. That means as an adult, you have the right not to see him."

"Yeah, you're right," Cori agreed.

"Of course, I'm right. When are you going to admit that I'm always right?"

Cori laughed. "I'm so lucky to still have you to advise me through all my life decisions."

Rosemary chuckled. "You never know when I might need to call in the favor at some point."

After she disconnected her call, but before she could send the text to Greg, there was a knock at her door. *Oh, don't let it be Greg.*

Her assistant's head popped through the open door. "Good morning. You're here early."

"Good morning, Merlene. I had a few things to take care of before the day started."

"You have flowers."

Cori groaned. "Don't I always have flowers? Don't bring these in, please."

"You want me to read the card?"

"No. Wait, yes. Go ahead." Cori prepared herself for more Greg drivel.

Marlene stepped away from the door and then returned with a vase full of sunflowers. She pulled out the card nestled in the blooms and read, "I will wait for you. You're worth waiting for. Dax."

Cori's breath left her lungs in a whoosh. She hadn't been expecting that. When had she told him how much she loved sunflowers? She must have. He remembered everything she had told him about herself.

And unlike all the arrangements from Greg, this one was simple and made of flowers she loved, rather than roses, which she hated.

Dax had remembered her preference.

Her heart swelled with....love? Maybe. What she knew was that she'd missed him terribly.

Her decision was made.

Dax was beautiful inside and out, even if he couldn't understand that was how she saw him. She needed to see where their relationship went.

"Bring the flowers in," she told her assistant. "Those I'll keep in my office."

"Your first appointment is here," Merlene said as she set the arrangement on Cori's desk.

"Thanks. Can you have them wait five minutes? I have something I have to do first."

"Sure."

Rosemary was right. Her problem was going to be solved by text.

Cori: *The flowers have been lovely and I enjoyed them. However, we have no future. I've moved on, and I'm very happy with my life. I've met someone else and I need to pursue that. There is no going back. I wish you luck and hope you find happiness in whatever path you take. After this message, I don't want to hear from you and will have blocked your number.*

Then she did what she said she was going to. She blocked the number.

Next, she found Dax's number and sent a text.

Cori: *I'm feeling like a Cowboy burger from Leo's Bar and Grill. Is Kobi available for a date?"*

Dax: *She is. However, her handler must come also.*

Cori: *Two for the price of one. That's my kind of bargain.*

Dax: *Can I pick you up? What time?*

Cori: *My office isn't all that far from Leo's. Pick me up here. About 5?*

Dax: *Sounds perfect. See you then.*

Before she could respond, another text from Dax arrived.

Dax: *I've missed you. I mean, Kobi missed you.*

Cori smiled. *Yeah. I missed Kobi (and her handler) too. See you at five.*

Cori floated through the rest of that day. She'd dealt with Greg's intrusion into her life and gotten back on track with Dax.

Her last appointment of the day was with Jack Rhett. There was something about the sixteen-year-old that brought out her maternal side. Life had certainly not been kind to him.

His entrance into her office followed his usual pattern. He slouched in, his hair hanging in his eyes, his gaze toward the floor. His clothes were clean, and she was glad to see that. She worried about his future. As a high school junior, he'd be on his own before he was ready. He flopped into his usual chair.

"Hey," he said, his voice deep and raspy.

"Hello, Jack. How are things going? Any fights I need to hear about?"

He shook his head, his long dark hair sliding from side to side with the action.

"I talked to your social worker this week. She says you still have problems getting along with Amos."

Amos and Lillian Vander were his current foster family. He'd been with them about a year.

His mouth tightened. "He's an asshole."

"In what way?"

For the hour, Jack talked about Amos, but also about high school and some of the bullies there.

Cori checked the time. Dax should be there in less than fifteen minutes. She needed to wrap this up.

"So, let me sum up our conversation," Cori said. "Everyone's an ass but you. You hate school because someone is always telling you what to do. You don't like Amos because he has rules and makes you follow them. The entire world is plotting against you. Have I got that about right?"

Jack's gaze bored into hers. "I can't wait to get out of school; then, nobody can tell me what to do."

Cori wanted to laugh. She remembered thinking

adulthood meant you were your own boss and rules no longer applied.

"Jack, I know your life had a rough start, and there's nothing I can do about that. But the life ahead of you? That's up to you. Life will always throw you curves, and you've got to be ready to change. Do you understand what I'm saying?"

As she waited for Jack to respond, multiple loud voices oozed under her door from her waiting room.

"I'm sorry, Jack. Hold on a minute."

When she opened her office door to see what was happening, she was surprised to see Greg standing in her office, along with Dax.

"Greg? What are you doing here? I made myself clear today," Cori said, her hands on her hips.

"Hear me out," Greg said. "Let me take you to dinner so we can talk."

"Nope," she said. "You can't be here for me. We're done."

"Not here for me," Merlene said, raising her eyebrows. "My husband objects to my having dates."

Dax snorted. "I don't want to have dinner with you so, you can't be here for me."

"Leave, Greg, before this gets out of hand," Cori said, pointing toward the exit. "Do not contact me again."

Dax glared at her ex, his posture rigid. "Man, read the room," he said, his voice deep and threatening. "You are not welcome, not now, not ever. Cori and I are dating." He glanced over to Cori.

"Dax and I are dating." She stepped over to where Dax stood. "Leave now, or I will call Sheriff Singer."

Greg moved as if he was going to advance toward Cori. Dax moved faster, whipping Greg's arm behind his back. He frog-marched her unwelcomed ex to the exit.

Merlene hurried over to open the door, and Dax walked Greg outside before he released his arm.

Twelve

The second Dax eased his hold on Greg's arm, he jerked it away and began rubbing his wrist.

In a low, threatening tone, Dax said, "Cori can take care of herself, but she doesn't have to. She has people who will stand with her and keep her safe. You are not welcome here. Do not come back. Do not contact her again. If you do, next time I won't be so nice."

"She'll be back," Greg sneered. "She always comes when I call."

The fact that Dax didn't smash his fist into this asshole's face was only because of the impressionable teen standing in Cori's office door. Her clients had enough troubles without him adding seeing violence to their plates.

"She told you to leave," Dax said. "Do it, or I'll call the sheriff, and believe me when I say, if I call, he will come personally."

Greg wheeled around and marched down the street.

Dax shook his head. When he reentered Cori's office, he overheard her telling the teen boy that violence was never the answer.

"She's right," Dax said.

Cori's gaze jumped from the teen to Dax.

"Don't mean to interrupt, but anytime you can avoid violence, do that. I wasn't being violent with that asshole." When Cori arched a brow at his choice of words, he changed directions quickly. "Er, jerk. No means no. No never means maybe, or the someone is playing hard to get. That, um, *jerk* was told no, and yet he wouldn't take a solid no for an answer." He shrugged. "I simply helped him find the door."

The teen boy's eyes were wide as he took in Dax. "Man, that was so awesome. Guy never knew what hit him." The boy stepped over to Dax. "I'm Jack Rhett."

"Dax Cooper."

"Where'd you learn that move? Are you a cop?"

Dax shook his head. "Army Ranger. Delta forces. Retired now."

"I bet you saw action, am I right?"

Dax assumed the kid—Jack—was looking at his scar tissue. "I saw some, yes."

"Where were you?" Jack asked.

Cori stepped over to where Dax and Jack stood. "Jack, I'm sure you have better things to do on a Friday night than to stand here and hear war stories."

Jack frowned. "Not really." He looked at Dax.

"What's the military like? Are you glad you did that? Were you always going to be in the Army? Why didn't you go to college?"

Dax chuckled. "Lots of questions, dude."

Cori placed her hand on Jack's shoulder. "Jack is trying to decide what he wants to do after high school."

"The military can be a good life, but it can be hard," Dax said.

"Why do you have a dog?" Jack asked, nodding toward Kobi.

Until that moment, Dax had actually forgotten about the golden retriever. She was sitting patiently beside the chair where Dax had told her to wait. How could he explain PTSD without sounding like a wimp? So, he went with the truth, but not the whole truth. "She belonged to a friend. When he died, he asked me to take Kobi and give her a home."

"Awesome," Jack said.

"Jack, do you need a ride home?" Cori asked.

"Huh? Oh, yeah. I can call Lillian to come pick me up."

"I'm sure we can drop you off, right, Dax?"

"Sure. Not a problem, although you'll have to give me directions. I don't know my way around. And you'll have to sit in the back with Kobi."

The teen grinned. "Dope."

Dax frowned. "Excuse me?"

Cori laughed. "It means he likes it," she explained.

Dax shook his head with a laugh. "I've never felt so old."

After dropping off Jack—and enduring a million military-related questions on the drive to his foster home—Dax was glad to finally have Cori alone. He took her hand as he drove to Leo's Bar and Grill.

"Finally," he said, "I've got you alone."

She laced their fingers. "I'm sorry about that scene in my office."

"It's not like you have much control over your ex."

"I know. I just feel horrible that both you and Jack were exposed to his toxicity. What did he say to you outside?"

"Doesn't matter." The asshole's comments still made him mad.

With a gentle squeeze, she said, "Whatever it was, it was bullshit."

"You better believe it was. Total crap." His jaw was tight with fury as he found a parking spot.

Cori ran her finger down his scarred cheek. "It's over," she said, stopping her finger under his chin. "I think I need a kiss to scrub today's memories from my brain."

The soft touch of her finger on his face sent his heart pounding while at the same time easing the tension in his shoulders. He smiled and leaned over the console. She met him halfway, their lips smashing together in a hungry, longing kiss. His tongue ran along the seam in her mouth, and she opened for him. Her tongue stroked his with long, erotic caresses. The kiss and tongue play continued for a while...maybe too long. Someone pounded on the hood of his truck, shouting, "Get a room."

Dax pulled back first and stared into Cori's dazed eyes. His were probably just as dazed with the lust and desire he saw reflected on her face.

"Sorry," he said. "I forget you're a well-respected psychologist in this town. I don't want to damage your reputation."

She dragged her thumb over his bottom lip. "I missed lunch, so I'm starving. If I weren't, we'd be headed to my house at top speed."

With a tortured sigh, he asked, "You're really hungry?"

Her stomach took that moment to grumble loudly.

He laughed. "I'll take that as a yes. Come on. I wouldn't want you to fade away."

Scoffing, she exited the truck. "Like that would ever happen." She slapped her hips. "I could stand to lose a few pounds."

"Don't do that," he said. "Don't say that about yourself." He put his arm around her. "Never run yourself down, at least not around me. I won't let you. You're perfect the way you are."

"You've never seen my sisters or my mother." She rolled her eyes. "I can't begin to compare to them."

His heart ached at her words. Sadly, he did understand. Didn't he compare himself to men with two functioning legs? His therapist would tell him not to discount Cori's feelings, but her opinion about herself was ridiculous, regardless of what her sisters and mother looked like.

They walked toward the entrance. "I had a thought about your comment, and I started to keep it to myself, but I don't think I will," he began. "I know you believe that you somehow aren't pretty, but honey, that's crazy. You are the sexiest, most incredible woman I've had the good fortune to date. I think you're beautiful."

She leaned heavily against him. "Thank you, Dax."

"It's true." He opened the door and let her enter Leo's first. As they entered, he heard someone shout Cori's name.

"Oh, I see some friends," she said. "I want you to meet them. Come on."

Dax allowed himself to be pulled across the bar to a four-top table with two couples sitting there. He prepared himself for the stares that would undoubtedly be aimed at his scars.

"Dax, these are my very best buds, Porchia and Magda. Porchia owns Heavenly Delights Bakery, and if you haven't already discovered it, you've made a huge mistake. Magda is the business manager for D&R Ranch." She gestured toward the men. "This is Reno Montgomery, the R in the ranch title. He's Magda's husband."

Reno extended his hand. "Nice to meet you, man."

"You too," Dax said, shaking his hand. He was excited to meet another extended family member, but he hated not being able to acknowledge their family ties. How had his brother lived here so long with telling the truth about their mother?

"And this is Darren Montgomery, the D in the ranch. He's married to Porchia."

Dax assumed Reno and Darren were first cousins, but he really needed Marc to draw him a family tree to see where everyone fit.

Darren patted his gut. "And that explains my extra ten pounds. Nice to meet you, Dax."

The two men shook hands.

"It's so good to meet you," Magda said. "We've heard so much about you."

"That's true," Porchia agreed.

Dax arched a brow. "Oh? What did she say?"

Cori glared at the woman. "You two need to zip it."

The two women laughed, obviously not in the least sorry or afraid of his date.

"Sorry, man. You don't want to tangle with these three," Darren said with a nod toward the two giggling women and the one woman glaring at her friends.

"Hmm, should I take that as a warning?" Dax asked, a smile wanting to break on his face, but he forced his face into a serious expression.

"Take it however you like," Reno said. "We've been around these three ladies for years, and they are trouble when they're together."

Dax laughed. "I kind of like trouble, but thanks for the warning. I'll bear it in mind."

Cori raised a finger. "One more introduction." She pointed toward the golden retriever sitting at Dax's fee. "This is Kobi."

"Oh my, Kobi. You're so beautiful," Porchia said, slipping off her stool. "Can I pet her, Dax?"

Dax glanced down at Kobi wearing her service vest. Dax shook his head. "No. Please don't. She's working." He gestured toward the dog's vest.

"Oh, gosh. Of course. I'm sorry," Porchia said.

"It's okay."

"So," Darren said, "you're Sheriff Singer's brother."

"Yeah. How'd you know?"

Reno laughed. "Oh man, have you not discovered the accuracy of the Whispering Springs rumor mill?"

Dax rolled his eyes. "Of course, I have. I don't know why I even asked that question."

"Y'all want to join us?" Reno asked. "We can pull up a table and some chairs."

Cori glanced at Dax for his response. Until his accident, being in crowds, especially crowded rooms, had never bothered him. Now, he felt claustrophobic and anxious in these environments. Kobi pressed against his leg.

"Thanks for the offer," Dax said, "but Kobi is more comfortable on the deck." When all other reasons fail, blame the dog.

"Got it," Reno said.

"Y'all come out later and join us for a drink before you head home," Cori invited.

"Sounds good, if that's okay with Dax," Porchia said.

Dax nodded. "See you guys later."

Dax and Cori were seated at a small table in the back corner of the deck. Private, but still outside. Dax felt like he could breathe out here.

Kobi dropped next to Dax's leg and put her head on his boot.

They both ordered cowboy burgers. Dax had a Coke and water. With his encouragement, Cori had a beer. When their server delivered their drinks, he also brought a bowl of fresh water for Kobi.

While they waited for their food, they chatted about nothing. It seemed that neither of them wanted to revisit today's show at the office.

"How are you getting along with Kobi?" Cori asked.

"Really good. My therapist agreed that I would do well with her."

Cori frowned. "You have a therapist? Here?"

"No, not here. He's based at Walter Reed in Washington and does a lot of work with injured vets. I still see him a couple of times a month via computer."

"Have you mentioned me? What has he said about dating?"

"He said I shouldn't date a psychologist because they're all nuts."

She laughed. "Well, he does have a point."

"Luckily for me, I adore nuts."

"Aww, thank goodness."

The food arrived, and Dax dug in. The Army didn't have hamburgers that tasted like this.

As he chewed his first bite, Cori said, "So, we're dating, are we?"

Dax pushed the hunk of food down his throat and chased it with a large gulp of water.

"Sorry," Cori said, but she didn't look the least bit sorry. "Did I catch you off-guard?"

He nodded. "How do you feel about that?" His heart raced as he waited for her reply. If she said no, he'd understand. He wasn't the biggest prize.

Cori put her elbow on the table and rested her chin in her hand. "I think I like it."

"I like it too," Dax said, relief washing over him. "But there's one thing you need to know."

"What's that?"

"I don't share."

"Share?"

"With others. Never have been good with sharing."

"Oh, I don't do *ménage à trois*."

He threw back his head in a loud laugh, his eyes tearing from laughing so hard. Taking her hand, he said, "That's not what I meant. I mean, exclusive dating. I want to date you and no other women. I don't want you to date other men either."

She snorted. "I knew what you meant, but hey..." She bumped his shoulder. "Never say never, and I don't want to date anyone else. I like being with you, Dax."

He smiled. "I like being with you too."

"So, we're exclusive?" Cori asked. "I just want to make sure I understand what we're talking about here. Just you and me. Nobody else. Right?"

He nodded. "Exclusive, yes."

"Good," she said. "I like that, but I have a question. It's a little intrusive."

"Go for it." He took another bite of his burger as he waited. She was taking a long time to ask whatever it was she wanted to know.

She sighed. "This is hard."

"No hurry. Take your time."

"The damage your body suffered...your scars...."

"Yeah, I've got scars you haven't seen. I told you that."

"No, no, that's not the question. Is there anything else I need to know about?"

He sighed and leaned heavily against the back of his chair. Setting his fork on the side of his plate, he said, "Yeah." He hiked his left pants leg to expose his artificial limb. "I'm missing part of my leg, from the knee down."

With a shrug, she said, "I know that."

"You did?"

"Well, I didn't know how much of your leg you'd lost, but I saw your prostheses the first night. You didn't mention it, so neither did I."

"And you haven't said anything about it?"

"What's there to say, and so what? But that isn't my question."

He frowned. "Okay, then what's the question."

"Is there anything else wrong that I need to know about?"

"I can see. I can taste. I can hear, although my hearing is a little damaged, but otherwise, I can't think of anything."

"Are you being deliberately obtuse?"

He laughed. "Not deliberately."

Her cheeks pinkened and she asked, "Can you have sex?"

His eyes opened wide. That was the last thing he'd expected her to ask. "Uh, are you asking if I have a penis and if it can get hard?"

She scowled. "Yeah, that's what I'm asking."

"Well, yeah," he said. "To both things. I have a cock, and yes, I can get a hard-on." He leaned closer and said, "And before you ask, I love sex. Really, really love sex."

"Whew, that's good news."

He grinned. "Oh, yeah?"

She pumped her eyebrows. "Oh, yeah. We might have to, um, check out the functionality of your cock later." Her eyes sparkled with a mischievous twinkle.

"Here we are," came a shout from across the deck.

Dax glanced over to see his two cousins—at least he thought Reno and Darren were probably his cousins—carrying a table closer. Porchia and Magda each carried two chairs.

He really needed a Montgomery family tree. He wasn't sure exactly how he was related to Reno and Darren, only that he was.

"We've got chairs and a table," Porchia announced in a sing-song voice.

"We want to get to know Dax better," Magda said, with a wink toward him. "Looks like he might be around a while."

Cori leaned toward her friends and whispered, "We might have been talking about sex. You ever think of that? Maybe this isn't the best time."

Magda howled. "Girl, you don't talk about sex— you have sex. Isn't that right, Dax?"

Reno shrugged. "We tried to warn you."

Dax was sure he had a deer-in-the-headlights look. How does one answer a question like that?

Thirteen

"Thanks for being a good sport with my friends," Cori said.

"I enjoyed meeting them. I can only imagine what trouble the three of you can find when left to your own devices."

Cori thought about the male stripper review that'd come to Dallas and Porchia just had to go to watch. Trouble had definitely been had that night. She smiled at the memory.

"You're ginning," Dax said. "Want to share what you're thinking about?"

"I do not," Cori replied, still feeling the amusement from her memories. Then to distract him from additional questions, she put her hand on his knee. Using one finger, she dragged her nail along the inside seam of his jeans, stopping short of directly touching his groin area. She then dragged her nail back down the seam. She continued this up-and-down motion,

Dax's eyes flickering from the road to where her hand lay on his thigh.

"Dr. Cora Belle Lambert. Are you trying to seduce me?"

"Is it working?"

"It's not failing," he said, turning into her drive.

She grinned. "Wanna come in? I have water."

"I could use a, um, drink of water."

Kobi was crashed out on the back seat, and Dax had to wake her to go inside Cori's house. Since this was the first time Dax had been inside her place, she was thankful her cleaning lady had come that day, leaving everything smelling fresh and clean.

The minute the door closed behind them; Dax pointed to the floor. "Go lay down," he said to Kobi. The retriever found a spot by a chair and dropped to the floor.

"Whew," Cori said. "I thought for a minute you were talking to me."

Dax caught her face between his large, warm hands, his thumbs gently stroking her cheeks. "If I thought it would work...." He pulled her head forward, and their mouths crashed together in a hot, passionate kiss.

Cori's breath mingled with his, her mouth open and receptive to his tongue. When he swept in, she sighed with pleasure. His kisses excited her heart and made her feel sexy and desirable.

She ran her palms down his chest, the hard muscles and angles acting as an aphrodisiac, sending lust pouring through her veins. She allowed her fingers to trace along the waistband of his jeans. Behind the zipper, he grew hard and rigid. Unable to resist the temptation, she raked her hand across that bulge. Her fingers traced his long, hard cock.

His breath caught. "Cori..." he growled, "you're playing with fire."

"No, I'm playing with your cock." She looked into his eyes. "And I would very much like to see what I'm feeling." She smiled shyly. This kind of bluntness wasn't her, but damn, she really wanted this man in her bed. What would he say about that if she blurted out her thoughts? Nervous he might leave if she voiced them, she held them tight in her mind.

"We should probably talk," Dax said and pulled Cori down to the sofa.

"What? Why? You obviously can get hard," she said with a grin as she stroked her hand over his jeans-covered cock.

Catching her hand, he pulled it to his mouth and kissed her knuckles. "Yeah, that's not the problem." He held her hand against his chest. "It's, um, been a while, if you get what I'm saying."

"Ah." She nodded. "When was the last time you had sex?"

"With someone other than my hand? Over two years."

"Damn," she said with a low whistle. "Of course, it makes sense, what with the injury and recovery."

"Yeah, so what I'm trying to say is...um..."

"You're a firecracker with a short fuse?" she suggested.

He chuckled. "Something like that."

"Is it bad that I love the idea that I'm going to be your first in a long time?"

"I'm not a virgin, Cori," he said with a grin.

"Hey! You have your fantasies, and I have mine," she said jokingly. She pulled her hand from his and unzipped his jeans, taking care over his ridged dick. "And Dax?" She looked up from where she'd been watching her own hand at work. "You are my fantasy."

His cock grew harder at her words, which had her insides exploding like a million rockets. She wiggled her fingers under the waistband of his briefs until she could wrap them around his dick. She squeezed, and the breath rushed from his mouth.

"Feel good?" she asked, squeezing, and then pumping her hand up and down.

"Fuck, yes," he said with a gasp. "I'm not going to last long."

"Well, then, let's not waste time." She lowered the waistband of his briefs, allowing his erect cock to spring out and into her hand. Not waiting for his reaction, she leaned over and lowered her mouth down his cock. His entire body stiffened, and he let out a long, low groan. His hips moved beneath her mouth, making her take him deeper. She hummed, making the back of her throat vibrate.

"Fuck," he muttered. "I'm not going to last long with your hot, luscious mouth around my dick."

Wrapping her fingers around the base of his cock, she stroked up as she slowly pulled her mouth up his long shaft. She ran her tongue around the rim before sliding back down.

"Cori, sweetheart, I can't take any more. I'm going to come."

Instead of stopping, as she suspected he meant for her to do, she got more vigorous sliding up and down. His fingers threaded into her hair and tightened. The sting from her hair being pulled sent her desire into orbit.

He let out a long, low groan, and shot hot semen into her mouth. She swallowed and then licked her way to the top.

"Take the edge off?" she asked with a grin.

His breathing was labored; his face flushed. "I think I died two years ago and this is heaven, right?"

She laughed. "Not hardly." She tucked him back into his briefs. "Stay the night," she said. "Make love to me."

His eyes, which had been closed, popped open and his gaze locked on hers. He shook his head. "I can't."

"Why? Give me one good reason and I'll drop it."

"Fuck, Cori, you know why I can't."

"Actually, I don't." She sat back on the sofa. "Explain it to me."

"Goddammit." He hoisted his left leg onto her coffee table and jerked up his pants leg. "There. That's why?"

She decided to stay obtuse, fairly sure she understood his hesitance. "Your prosthesis? Take it off, if it's bothering you."

"Stop it, Cori," he demanded roughly. "That's not going to happen."

With a forced frown and arched brow, she said, "We are going to be lovers, right? You do want to have sex with me, don't you?"

"Of course, I want to be lovers. I don't have to take this off to do that."

"I see. So, you can be in my mouth and in my body, but removing your artificial leg and me seeing your stump is too intimate? Have I got that right?"

He glared at her.

She glared back, her look more of a challenge than one of frustration. Of course, she knew he didn't have to take it off to make love. She'd been doing some reading about below-the-knee amputations (aka BKA), and it was safe to keep the leg on. However, she wanted him to feel her full acceptance of him in his current situation. The scars. The prosthesis. Everything about him was beautiful to her. She wanted no questions in his mind.

"I'd better go," he said, standing.

"Dax." She caught his hand. "Don't go. I see your scars. I see your artificial leg and I think you're incredible. I see that you're beautiful inside and out."

He looked down to where she remained seated on the sofa. "You don't have to say that."

Standing, she smiled. "I know I don't, but it's the truth. You may not see yourself as I do." She put her hand on his chest. "I want you to stay. I want to explore these feelings I think we share. I don't want anything hidden from each other." She sighed. "We both have scars, Dax. You just haven't seen mine."

He frowned. "Where? Your face is flawless. Your body drives me crazy. I can't see a thing wrong with you."

"I have a big scar on my butt."

Surprise flickered on his face. "What happened?"

With a snort, she said, "A horse bit me. I had a bunch of stitches and couldn't sit on that side for a month. And yeah, before you made the joke, I was the butt of everyone's jokes at school, not to mention my sisters teased mercilessly. Just because you can't see it doesn't mean it isn't there and doesn't bother me.

"I'm sorry." He sat back beside her.

"When others see your scars, they know you've been through something serious. Your scars tell people you are a warrior, and I believe you have a warrior's heart. What's hard are the scars that can't be seen, the ones in your soul. Those hurt sometimes worse than physical ones." She sighed. "I'd love for you to meet my parents, but I'm nervous about taking you home. Not because of your scars or your leg," she hurried to add, "but because I don't want you to meet my sisters. Elsie and Annabelle are beautiful like swans, regal and gorgeous. Beside them, I look like a wet squirrel."

For the first time in a while, a smile crossed his mouth. "That's ridiculous."

"No, it's true. Throughout my dating years, guys would ask me out so they could get close to my sister,

Elsie. Annabelle was too young to date back then, although, those days are past. She's eighteen, so..." She rubbed at the ache in her heart with these memories. "I've been dumped more than once by a guy who wanted Elsie more. So, there's my truth. I have insecurities about my appearance."

Dax wrapped his arm around her shoulders and pulled her against his chest. "You tell me I'm beautiful, and at one point in my life, I would've believed you. Now? Naw. I have mirrors, Cori."

"Fine, you're not pretty. You're handsome, inside and out." She looked up into his eyes. "I see your pain, but I also see your strength."

Hugging her tightly, he said, "You are so beautiful to me."

"Then you'll stay? We'll not erect walls between us?"

"It's not pretty, Cori."

"I'm not scared of anything you will show me," she said. "Well, your cock was pretty damn big, and that was scary."

He was chuckling as she took his hand and led him down the hallway to her bedroom.

Beatrice was stretched across the bed in all her cat glory and rolled onto her back when they walked in.

"You have a cat," Dax said.

"Oh, are you allergic?"

"I don't think so. I've just never been around one."

Their conversation was interrupted by Kobi's

arrival in the room. She walked over to the bed and studied Beatrice.

"Kobi, this is Beatrice. Beatrice, this is Kobi. Be nice," Cori said.

Beatrice eyed the dog, stood, flipped her tail in the air, jumped off the bed, and strode from the room.

Kobi seemed nonplussed by the interaction and found a place by the dresser to curl up.

"That went better than I'd feared," Cori said. In a whisper, she added, "Beatrice is kind of a bitch."

Dax chuckled. "Kobi was trained to not get distracted when on the job, so I guess bitches fall into that category."

"Good," Cori said. "I like to hear you laugh. I love your smile. It makes my heart happy."

She stepped back and stripped her shirt over her head. Then, she shimmied her pants down her legs, leaving her dressed in only a bra and a pair of panties. Turning toward Dax, she walked over with a confidence she didn't feel, and began to unbutton his shirt.

"Cori," he said, catching her hands in his.

"Dax." His heart was pounding under her hands. His eyes were dilated, and his breathing ragged. "If you can look me in the eye and tell me you don't want me, or you don't want to be in my bed, then I'll stop, and you can go home."

His broad hands dropped hers and caught both her ass cheeks in his palms. His fingers slipped under the leg elastic and dug into her flesh. "You're not playing fair."

She finished unbuttoning his shirt and slid her hand down his flesh. "I'm not playing, Dax. I'm deadly serious."

He studied her face and must have decided she was serious. His face relaxed marginally. "Can we start with the scars?"

Pushing his shirt off his body, she leaned forward and pressed her lips to his scar tissue. "We can start there." She kissed all over the scarred tissue. Through it all, she felt his heart pounding rapidly beneath her lips.

With an ease that amazed her, he lifted her off her feet and set her on her bed. He looked at her for so long Cori got twitchy.

"I want to see your scar," he said with low, rough voice. "You've seen mine."

She got on her knees and turned her back toward him. Lowering only one side of her panties to expose the oval scar, she looked over her shoulder. "Ugly, isn't it?"

He ran the tip of his index finger around the scar. "This bothers you? It's kind of cute."

She turned back around. "It's not how it looks, I guess. It's the bad memories it stirs up." She touched his upper arm. "What's this?"

"Bullet scar."

She winced. "And this?" She touched another spot.

"Shrapnel from the IED. Most of these scars are either shrapnel or bullets."

"Those fuckers," she muttered and began kissing each spot.

He pressed the side of her head against his chest. "You can do better than me, honey. I'm a broken-down vet with an uncertain future."

She pulled back until their gazes met. "Better, as in, without scars? With better skin? With two legs? Is that what you mean? Because I call bullshit. Greg had great skin. Handsome face. Two legs. Two arms. And there's no way you can tell me you think he's better than you. No, sir. You're the one I want. You're right for me."

On her knees, their mouths were close to the same height. He leaned in and kissed her. "You're the one I want too, Cori."

Her heart swelled with emotion. Love? Too early to use that word, but she felt confident their future would be filled with love.

Cori slipped off the sheets and stood. "Sit." She pointed at the mattress.

Dax sat.

Kneeling at his feet, she untied his shoes. She could feel tension and anxiety coming off him in waves. She reached for the shoe on his natural foot and looked up at him. "Honestly, I'm more worried about toe jam than seeing your stump."

He laughed, and she would have sworn she could hear the relief in the sound. "No toe jam," he said, an amused expression on his face. "I showered and everything."

She grinned up at him. "Whew." She slipped his shoe and sock from his foot. When she reached for the artificial limb, he stiffened. "Am I the first female who's seen your stump...other than medical personal?"

"Yes, other than my mother."

"Ah, well, mothers are granted a lot of rights." She removed the shoe and then the sock, exposing the foot. In all her reading about artificial legs, she couldn't remember what the foot was made of, but it'd been designed to look like a foot with toes. "Great looking foot." She stood and wedged herself between his thighs. Slipping her arms over his shoulders and around his neck, she asked, "You doing okay?"

His Adam's apple bobbed up and down as he swallowed. "I'm okay."

She kissed him hard and long before pulling back. "Let's tackle those jeans." She unfastened his belt and popped the metal rivet at the waist. Then, she carefully lowered the zipper over a cock she knew had an impressive length and width. He lifted his hips off the mattress, and she slid the heavy denim down his legs and over his feet. She was surprised at the length of his artificial limb. It was so much shorter than she'd expected.

"Is something wrong?" he asked when she got quiet.

"Not at all. I'm very good. I've fondled your thigh muscles, so I knew your prosthesis didn't go above the knee." The prosthesis started in the lower part of his fibula and tibial, and encompassed his ankle and foot. "Can we take it off?"

Leaning over, he pressed a button that released the device. After removing it, he slid off the sock with the locking pen, leaving his exposed stump.

She ran her hand down his leg and cupped the end of his leg. There was scarring, but not as extensive as she'd thought it would be. "Does it hurt if I touch it?"

He shook his head. "Not any more. Initially, hell yeah, but it's healed up."

She placed a kiss on the stump, and raised her gaze to his. "I'm so glad you're here and with me." She joined him on the mattress. "Make love to me, Dax."

Their lovemaking was unlike anything she'd experienced before. She wasn't the most experienced lover, as she'd only been with four guys, but tonight was different. The entire experience with Dax was special. They'd make love, sleep, and come together again. When the morning came, Cori's feelings were no longer scattered. They were solid and deep for him. She could only hope he felt the same.

The next day, she had to go to her parents' house for a late lunch without Dax. He had made plans with his brother, but his evening was free, or was free until Cori filled it for him. Dinner at her house. She would cook. He left and she floated on air all morning.

As she turned into her parents' drive, she drew in

a deep breath. She loved the rural areas of the county...the grass waving in the breeze, the rustle of the wind through the pine trees, and especially the calves running to keep up with their mothers. Outside was her comfort zone. Indoors made her cranky.

"Why are you so happy?" Elsie asked her when she climbed from her car. Elsie was, as usual, sitting on the front porch, a martini in her hand.

"Just in a good mood. What are you doing here? Shouldn't you be home with your husband?"

"Someone has to make sure Annabelle is stunning tonight for the prom."

The insult hit Cori directly in the chest, as it was meant to. The urge to respond in kind was beaten back by her good mood. Even her older sister couldn't make her grumpy. Instead of replying, Cori laughed as she walked past her and into the house.

"I'm here and starving," she called out.

"In the kitchen," her mother replied.

"Smells good," Cori said after hugging her mom.

"Roast with mashed potatoes, green beans, corn on the cob, and rolls."

"Yum."

"Round up the rest of the family so we can eat. I can only imagine how long it's going to take Annabelle to get ready for tonight."

"What time is Noah picking her up?"

"About six-thirty. There's a group going to dinner at Rick's on the River before the prom."

It took Cori fifteen minutes to corral her family to the table.

As they were serving themselves, her father said, "I heard the Hanson place sold."

Cori thought of Dax and their date and was sad the old ranch had been bought. She guessed stargazing in the field won't happen again.

"You'll never guess who bought it," he said.

"Sheriff Singer and his brother," her mother said. "You know you'll never get the gossip before me."

Her dad chuckled. "Yes, dear," he said sarcastically. "I would have love to have that piece of land, but the family had their own ideas." He took a bite of roast. "I wonder how the sheriff could afford it? The asking price was well over two million, and that wasn't unreasonable given its location."

"Dax bought that land?" Cori asked.

"Him and his brother," her mom replied.

"Why did you tell me?"

"It just happened, honey. I talked to Hillary Hillerman, who had the listing. She said the papers were signed on Thursday, so you're not so far behind on the Whispering Springs grapevine news."

"I'm just surprised Dax didn't tell me."

"Oh? You've seen him again?" her mother asked.

Before Cori could answer, Elsie said, "I saw Greg Simmons this week. He says he's moving home." Elsie snickered as she said, "He claims to have come back to convince you to marry him."

"Did you mention what he planned to do about his wife and children?"

Elsie shrugged. "Divorce, I imagine. He didn't say, and I didn't ask. But he's still quite handsome, don't you think?"

"I don't think about him at all," Cori replied.

"So, I shouldn't be looking for a dress to wear to your wedding?" Elsie asked, lifting her martini glass to her mouth.

"I think not." Cori's phone vibrated in her pocket, and she pulled it out. "Excuse me. I need to take this call." Stepping away from the table, she answered, "Hey, Dax."

"I'm not catching you at a bad time, am I?"

Her heart sped up at the sound of his voice. She really, *really*, liked how deep and sexy it was. "Nope. Perfect timing. What's up?"

"Did I see your car at your parents' house?"

"Yes, sir. Having lunch. You hungry?"

He chuckled. "I'm always hungry. Marc and I are over at the Hanson Ranch. I totally forgot to tell you that we bought it, but I was distracted last night."

"Yeah? A good distraction?" A smile bloomed on her lips.

"The best distraction." He cleared his throat. "Hold on."

She heard him yelling that he'd be there in a minute, and then he was back.

"Sorry about that. Marc was calling me. He's crazy excited."

"I'm happy for you. Are both of you going to live in the Hansons' old house?"

"God, no. I plan to build a new house. Marc

wants to renovate their house from top to bottom and live there. I'm happy to give him that. Anyway, the reason I'm calling, besides to remind you about dinner tonight, I thought you might want to come over and look around with me, maybe help me pick a spot for my house."

"Heck, yeah. I'll be over in about fifteen minutes." She clicked off and had to calm her racing heart and excited breathing before she went back to her parents' table. There was nothing her mother would love more than to believe she'd set her daughter up on a date with the perfect man.

Nope. Can't give Clover Lambert an ounce of a hint.

Fourteen

"Cori's coming over," Dax said to Marc. "Why?"

"Um, I invited her."

"Am I seeing a blooming romance?" Marc joked.

"Maybe."

His brother looked surprised. "Seriously? You're falling for Cori Lambert?"

Dax shrugged. "She's pretty cool."

"But you haven't known her all that long."

"I'm thirty-six, Marc, not sixteen. I know what I like in a woman."

Marc nodded. "I suppose you do. Mom will get a kick out of being responsible for setting you up with a woman you fall for."

"God, don't tell her."

Marc laughed. "My lips are sealed. Now, have you thought about where you want to build?"

"Not yet. I thought I'd ask Cori what she thinks."

That caused Marc's eyebrows to shoot up. "Getting the little woman's approval?"

Dax's punch to Marc's shoulder was his reply to that comment. "You know," he said, "I've been thinking and you're not going to like what I'm going to say."

Marc frowned. "What?"

"It's time, Marc. We need to meet with Mom's brothers. I can't live with this hanging over my head for the rest of my life. If I'm going to settle here, I have to clear the air with the Montgomerys." Even as Dax said settle here, his mind stubbornly refused to let go of the option to leave. However, after last night with Cori, his desire to move on had been severely diminished.

"Fuck," Marc said on a long exhale.

"I know," Dax said. "I think you're wrong that they will get you removed as sheriff, but if that happens, I'll be here to help you face the consequences. But we don't want to face the entire Montgomery clan without them knowing the situation. Monday is Memorial Day and Cori mentioned me going with her to some big deal party they always hold that day, I'd like to see if Lane and Clint can meet with us tomorrow."

"That's fast," Marc said, frowning.

"I know, but we need to rip off the bandage."

The sound of tires on the gravel caught their attention. Dax felt the corners of his mouth wanting to pull into a smile. That had to be Cori.

"Call them and set it up," Dax said.

Marc nodded. "Fine. Not thrilled, but I'll do it."

"Dax? Y'all in the house?" Cori called from the yard.

"Set it up," Dax repeated before heading to the front door to meet Cori.

"Hey, handsome," she said, putting her arms around his neck and pulling him to her for a kiss.

"Hey, beautiful."

"Hello, Cori," Marc said. "Good to see you."

"Hi, Marc," Cori said. "So, let's see what you two have gotten yourselves into."

They walked around the immediate area as Marc showed her the barn and other outbuildings. He then went into exacting details concerning the renovations he planned for the house. From the specifics Marc spouted, it was obvious he'd given many hours of thought to this reno. Dax made mental notes on everything Marc wanted. Being able to remodel the house into Marc's vision for the place would give Dax a lot of joy.

Cori agreed with Marc that Cash Montgomery was the main go-to guy for projects like this.

The rest of the day, Dax thought about his family. Not his mom and dad in Maine, but the extended family here in Whispering Springs. He'd toyed with the idea of meeting them without their knowledge of who he was ever since Marc had moved to Texas.

The more he thought about it, the more it didn't make sense that his mom hadn't been screaming bloody murder at Marc for being in Texas, nor did her arranging a blind date for him here in her hometown make sense.

Now, with their sister joining them, the dam of secrets was bursting at the seams. And tomorrow was the day the dam would break.

No matter what happened with his extended family tomorrow, Cori needed to know everything. Hadn't they promised no walls? No secrets?

That evening as they ate her homemade pizza—which was incredible and he could fall in love with her for that alone—Dax decided telling Cori first might gauge the community's reaction to the news.

Setting his slice of pizza on his plate, he said, "I need to tell you something."

Cori set her pizza down, drained the beer in her glass, and said, "Okay. I'm beer fortified, so hit me with it."

Dax's stomach was nervous, gastric acid seemed to splash up the sides.

His face must have looked so serious because Cori reached over and took his hand. "Whatever it is you want to tell me, Dax, I can handle it. Trust me to have your back."

"I haven't been completely honest with you about my family."

She nodded slowly and pulled her hand back to her side of the table. "I understand. Family dynamics can be touchy."

"Not my immediate family," he explained. "Marc, Sami, and I are tight with our parents. It's my extended family."

"A group of cattle rustlers and thieves?" she said with a grin.

He chuckled. "I don't think so, but then you'd know them better than I do."

"Oh, God, don't tell me that we're first cousins or something."

With another chuckle, he said, "Not that I know of." He took a drink of water to help his dry throat. "My mom was, well is, a Montgomery. Lane and Clint Montgomery are her brothers."

Cori's eyes opened wide. "Oh, my goodness. The infamous missing sister."

This time, it was Dax's turn to be surprised. "You've heard of my mom?"

"Of course. Everyone here has heard about the big family spat and your mom's leaving. She and my mother were best friends in—oh my God—my mother and your mother." She slapped her forehead. "How did I not see this? They're not just friends online who set up their kids on a date. They're childhood best friends who set up their kids. I'm going to have a long talk with my mother. I bet she's known where your mother was all these years and kept that information from her brothers."

"If you're right—and let's face it, it does make sense—then your mom only did what my mom asked her to. It had to be hard on her to keep that secret for so many years."

"Are you going to tell the Montgomery clan about your mom?"

He nodded. "Marc and I are meeting with Lane

and Clint tomorrow. Sami is in Dallas at the police academy and can't get away tomorrow, so it's just the two of us facing them. I hope I don't screw up Marc's future as sheriff here."

"Why would this mess with Marc's job?" Cori asked with a frown. "Marc was elected to his office, not appointed. Plus, I can tell you that he's quite popular with the citizens."

"And the Montgomerys wield a lot of power in this area. With a few choice words to the right people, Marc would be toast."

"They wouldn't do that."

Dax shrugged. "I don't know them. I don't know what they're capable of."

She laced her fingers in his. "I know the Montgomerys. Remember, I'm friends with Magda and Porchia and their husbands." Her mouth dropped into an O. "That means Reno and Darren are your first cousins."

He nodded.

"And you knew that when we had drinks at Leo's."

He nodded again.

"Wow. That must've been awkward. I'm so sorry for putting you in that situation."

"Not your fault. It's more my mom's fault for starting this whole situation to begin with. Besides, it was nice to get to know my cousins."

"Do you want me to go with you tomorrow to meet with Lane and Clint, just for moral support?"

Her suggestion touched his heart. "That's sweet, but no. We have to do this ourselves."

"Well, I'll be here waiting for you when you're done. Regardless of their reaction, I'm glad you're here." She leaned toward him and he met her halfway. They kissed over the table. "And I'm glad my mom's a sneak who set me up with her best friend's son."

"I wonder why they didn't try to set you up with Marc? I mean, he's been here a while?"

"Age difference maybe? I don't know, but I'll ask."

"No, don't do that. You wouldn't like living with him. He's a neat freak."

"And you're not?" She gestured to where his napkin was folded precisely beside his chair.

"Military training," he said.

"Hmm."

He stayed the night at Cori's. This time, he'd brought a small overnight bag and Kobi's bed and food. When he'd been getting things together, he'd felt giddy like a college kid sneaking over to his girl-friend's house from his parents' house. Marc had raised an eyebrow as Dax and Kobi had left, but he hadn't said anything. Dax would have sworn, however, that Marc was fighting a smile.

The next morning, he and Kobi headed to the Bar M Ranch. They were meeting Marc there. He was on call for the department since his main deputy sheriff was on vacation, and he could be called away suddenly. Dax hoped that didn't happen before, or during, their meeting. This was going to be hard enough for Dax. Without his brother, or sister, his PTSD might raise its ugly head.

His stomach was in knots as he turned into the drive of the Bar M and stopped at the gate. He rang the buzzer and announced himself. The electric gate swung open, and he passed under the arched sign. Everything about this place screamed success. The concrete drive. The waving fields of grass with cattle idly munching or laying about. Trucks with various company names lined the drive. He assumed preparations for tomorrow's Memorial Day event were in full swing.

Marc's sheriff-labeled SUV was parked in the drive close to the front door. Dax was relieved to see Marc exiting the vehicle as he drove up.

"Good timing," Marc said.

"Glad I didn't beat you here."

"Ready?"

"Nope, but lead on." Dax got Kobi from his truck and followed his brother to the door.

"Sheriff Singer," the woman who answered the door said. "Lane and Clint are on the patio managing the party setup." She leaned toward them to stage whisper, "That means they're drinking and watching."

Marc laughed. "Thanks, Jackie. This is my brother, Dax Cooper. Dax, this is Jackie Montgomery, Lane's wife."

To Dax's surprise—more like shock—the woman hugged him. "I've heard all about you."

Dax chuckled. "And I know all about the

community grapevine. Seems it's faster and more accurate than any U.S. spy agencies."

Jackie laughed. "Probably been around about as long."

She looked down at Kobi. "And this must be Kobi. She's beautiful."

"Thank you."

"Well, come on." As she led them through the house, she said, "The outdoor kitchen is fully stocked. Make yourselves at home when you get outside." She opened one side of a set of French doors. "Lane, Marc and Dax are here."

The two men, Lane and Clint, had their heads together chatting and pointing. At Jackie's voice, both men turned toward the door.

Dax's nerves ramped up to twelve on a scale of one to ten. He'd long ago given up his cane, but at this moment, he wished he had something to lean on. Two men with his mother's face stared back at him. How did Marc not crack seeing Mom's face on her brothers every time he had to deal with them?

One of the men stood and extended his hand to Dax. "I'm Lane Montgomery. You must be Dax." As they shook hands, he gestured toward the other man. "And this is Clint."

"Nice to meet both of you," Dax said, his voice steadier than he felt.

"Good to see you, Marc," Lane said.

"You too, sir. Clint. You doing good?"

"I am. Thank you, Marc."

"You boys grab something to drink and join us. We are heavy at work getting ready for tomorrow."

Marc chuckled. "I can see that. I hope our visit isn't inconvenient."

"Not at all," Lane said. "We're a little curious why you've asked to see us." He tilted his head. "Kitchen is stocked. Help yourself."

After Marc had his cold Coke and Dax had pulled out a bottle of water, they joined their uncles. Dax settled Kobi on a rug in the shade.

"Cheers," Clint said and lifted his beer.

They all drank, although Dax had difficulty getting the water around the boulder in his throat.

"Well, this is an awkward situation," Marc said.

Dax leaned forward. "My moving to Whispering Springs has made a long-kept secret no longer easy to keep."

Lane exchanged glances with Clint. "Secrets, huh? Well, at my advanced age, I've found that blurting it out is usually the best."

"Our mom is Cora, your sister," Marc said. "I didn't mean to deceive you or hide the truth from you. I didn't come here to cause problems or upset you in any way."

Their uncles' expressions shuttered.

"We've always known Mom had family down here," Dax said. "She didn't talk about it much. Whenever we brought it up, she seemed to get upset, so we stopped asking."

"I doubt we've talked about Mom's childhood in twenty years," Marc continued. "We let it drop, and so did she. Unfortunately, Dax, Sami, and I remained curious, like kids who know there's a secret, and we just had to find out what it was. Oh, Sami is Samantha, our sister."

Lane and Clint were nodding and listening, not going overboard with their reactions, which calmed Dax's nerves...some.

"I moved here to find out about Mom's family," Marc explained. "I didn't intend to stay as long as I have, but I fell in love with the people and area and found it impossible to leave."

"Then," Dax picked up the story, "after I finished rehab—an IED almost took me out—I came down to get away from Mom. Don't get me wrong," he hurriedly added. "Mom is fabulous, but she was smothering me with her love. I guess when one of your kids has a brush with death, you get to do that. Anyway, I showed up here and stirred up the mud."

"After Dax had been here a day or so, our sister Sami arrived on my doorstep," Marc said.

As Dax and Marc talked, Lane and Clint's heads swung back and forth like they were watching a tennis match.

"All of us have been separated for years," Marc continued. "Military and deployments had us all over the world. I guess we got a little lonely for family."

"Sami jumped in to moving here with both feet," Dax said. "When Marc wouldn't hire her on at the sheriff's department staff, she got a job with the Whispering Springs Police Department."

"Now that all of Cora Montgomery's children

are living in her hometown, we felt it was only right you knew who we were, and most importantly, we don't mean to intrude on your lives," Marc finished.

Lane and Clint exchanged looks that reminded Dax so much of his mother, he momentarily missed her.

Lane, the older of the Montgomery siblings, nodded. "Yes, we know."

Marc's mouth dropped open. "What? You know, as in you already knew my mom was your sister?"

"That's right," Clint said. "We've known for quite some time."

"How?" Dax asked.

"Don't you boys have mirrors? You look like your mother—Marc more than you, Dax. And Marc, when you ran for sheriff, you don't think we didn't have you checked out before we supported your run?" Lane said. "Our family has a lot of financial investments in this county. We weren't going to put our name and our resources behind a man we barely knew." He shrugged. "So, in a nutshell, we had you investigated."

"I can say we weren't all that surprised to have our suspicions confirmed," Clint said. "As Lane mentioned, you look like your mom. We liked the idea that our nephew was going to be sheriff."

Marc's eyes were wide, and he wore a stunned expression.

"I don't get it," Dax said. "If you knew who he was, that means you've known where your sister—

our mother—was all this time and you never contacted her?"

"Who says we didn't contact her?" Lane snapped. "Of course, we did, right, Clint?"

"Damn straight. We were happy to discover she was married and a college professor. Damned impressed. So, Marc's coming here and us finding Cora was a double blessing."

"Why the hell haven't you said anything?" Marc bit out. "I've walked on eggshells for years, concerned that you'd discover my background."

"We talked about it," Lane said.

"But," Clint continued, "we decided you had your reasons for not coming to us. We thought it best to let you live your life as you wanted. We've welcomed you into our homes on lots of occasions. We would've welcomed you into the family if you'd given any indication you wanted that."

Lane chuckled and looked at Dax. "At one point, your brother was dating my son's future wife. That was quite the pickle, right, Clint?"

Marc looked chagrinned.

"Marc?" Dax asked.

"I went out with Paige, Cash's wife. They weren't married or anything. I'm not even sure they were dating."

"Yes, well, you lit a fire under my son's ass," Lane said with a laugh. "Cash was ready to come to fisticuffs with you over Paige. Maybe I should thank you for getting him on the right path with her."

"Nothing happened with Paige," Marc said a little defensively.

"Oh, we know," Lane said. "If there had, I think blood would have been spilled."

Dax blew out a long breath. "So, you're okay with us being here?"

"Of course, we are," Clint said. "We're glad to have Cora's branch back where it belongs."

"How do you think the rest of the family will take this news?" Dax asked, concerned that the cousins might not be as thrilled as their uncles.

"Oh, they took it fine," Lane said.

"Wait," Marc said. "They *took* it fine? You mean they know?"

Lane nodded. "Ever since Cash and Paige got together. We told Cash who you were so he wouldn't run over you with his truck. He can't keep a secret if his life depends on it, so the news spread through the rest of the family faster than the usual grapevine speed."

Marc ran his hand through his hair. "Wow. I mean, I'm shocked. How did I not know? How did this not spread through the town?"

"We protect our own," Lane said simply. "You're ours, so you fall under Montgomery protection. Did you not think it odd we invited you to every Montgomery function, including the family camping trips?"

"I...I...I thought you invited me because I was the sheriff."

"And before that, you were only a deputy with no power," Lane said.

Marc gave a low whistle. "Guess I'm not as good a detective as I thought."

Lane and Clint chuckled.

"Naw, you're good." Lane patted his brother's back. "We're just sneakier."

Dax dropped his hand over the side of his chair and snapped his fingers. Kobi hurried over and shoved her head into his hand. His anxiety and nerves were making him get tense. Coming clean should have cleared the air, but he was still bugged.

"How long have you known where your sister was?"

The Montgomery brothers looked at each other, and Clint quirked the corners of his mouth up. "About a month after she left."

"How?" Dax asked his fingers stroking Kobi.

"Bless Clover Belle Lambert. She told us. In fact, she kept us in the loop about where your mother was at all times. When your father died, Marc, the funeral was paid for by the company he worked for, even though that company never had, nor ever will again, pay for a funeral. When your mom went to college, she was lucky to qualify for all those grants nobody had ever heard of which enabled her to graduate without debt. We loved your mom with all our hearts. We were considerably older and should have, could have, handled the situation better. But she didn't want us in her life, so we intervened in ways that would help her without upsetting her."

Dax sighed. "Anytime we tried to talk to her about her family, she'd get upset." He glanced at Marc. "To tell you the truth, we don't really understand what happened. Why did Mom leave?"

Lane's face grew sad. "This is how we see what happened. Your mom's version could vary slightly from ours. Clint and I are much older than your mom. When our parents died, Cora was only eighteen. She'd been the only child still living at home for most of her life. Their deaths were a heavy emotional blow to her. Clint and I had both already married and were starting families of our own. Cora was seeing this guy who had dollar signs in his eyes whenever he came out to the ranch. He convinced her that since she was the only daughter, and the only offspring living at home, she was entitled to the ranch as the sole heir. When she was told no, and the estate was ultimately divided into thirds, she got angry and ran away with this guy."

He glanced at Clint, who picked up the story. "We've always thought that this guy talked her into leaving, hoping to pressure us into giving her a larger portion of the estate. When we didn't, he left her stranded in California. She could have come home at that point, but you know how teens can be. She'd drawn her line in the sand and, we believe, was too embarrassed to admit what she'd done was, well, childish. It wasn't long after that she met your dad, Marc, and they married. We reached out to her about that time, but she was still hurt and angry. She told us to leave her alone. Your dad, Marc, was a great guy, and we've always believed that had he lived, this family would have reconciled years ago. But his death and your birth seemed to harden her heart. So, we watched from afar and tried to do what we could for her, like paying for her college with scholarships and grants."

"What happened to her third of the estate?" Dax asked.

"It's in the bank. That's where the money came from for school. After that, we invested it as we did our own." Lane chuckled. "Your mom has a nice nest egg waiting on her."

"So, what do you want to do now?" Marc asked. "I'm okay if you want to continue the ruse in the public eye. Less drama. Less gossip."

"Yeah, you know that isn't how this is going to work." Lane stood and walked over to where Dax and Marc sat. He put an arm around the shoulder of each of them. "I would love to claim you as my nephews. I'm proud of you, Marc. The respect you've won from the town without our assistance shows the Montgomery blood runs deep in you." He turned to Dax. "And you, Dax. You served our country with such honor and devotion. I couldn't be prouder if I were your own father."

Clint joined Lane beside the men. "We discussed this before you got here, wondering if family would be the topic for this visit. We would like to introduce you to the community during the party tomorrow. How would you feel about that?"

Marc cleared his throat. "This hasn't gone like I

thought it would at all." He looked at their uncles. "I thought you might be pissed and run me out of town. Instead, you're making sure I stay."

"You and Dax and Sami, if we can," Lane said.

"I'd be honored," Marc said.

"And you, Dax?"

Dax looked at Marc. "What will Mom say about all this?"

"You can ask her yourself. She'll be here tomorrow," Lane said.

Fifteen

Dax and Kobi got into his truck as Marc climbed back into the Sheriff's Department SUV. Dax blew out the long breath he'd held for the last hour.

"Mom will be here tomorrow," he told Kobi. "We need to warn Cori and give you a bath."

At the word bath, Kobi whined and hid her face under her paw, a trick David had taught him.

"I know, I know," Dax told the dog as he drove out of Bar M ranch. "But let's face it, buddy. First impressions count."

As though she understood every word, Kobi sighed and dropped onto the seat.

Dax headed for Cori's house, hoping she was home. She'd mentioned going by her folks' house to see how her sister's prom had gone. However, her car was in the drive when he got there. He pulled in and parked.

Before he could get his driver's door open, Cori

opened her front door and stood in the opening, waiting for him. His heart swelled so large he could barely breathe. She was so gorgeous. So wonderful. How in the hell had he gotten so lucky? Damn, in addition to his mom's help during his medical recovery, he was going to owe her double for putting Cori into his life. Honestly, looking at her, he'd gladly pay every day for the privilege of having her with him.

Was he in love?

She smiled at him, and his heart melted in his chest.

He was. Totally and completely. Cora Belle Lambert was his perfect match.

Did she feel the same?

"Dax, that sounds like a great visit," Cori said. "I made Mom confess that she knew who you were, who Marc was." She chuckled. "Mom cannot keep a secret. I'm proud of her for keeping this one, even if she did tell Cora's brothers everything. If you haven't guessed, I was named after your mom. Until today, I had no idea why mom gave me the name Cora. Don't be mad, but I kind of hated my name...until today." She smiled broadly. "Now that I know where it came from, I'm so proud of it."

Dax's arm was around her shoulders, and he pulled her tighter so they could snuggle. "I think I'll stick with Cori if you don't mind. Using my mom's name in the throes of passion might weird me out."

Cori laughed. "I can see that!"

"'*Oh, Cora, you make me so horny*'," Dax joked. "That geeks me out."

Cori howled with laughter. "Don't do that again."

Dax grinned. "You're going with me to the Memorial Day party tomorrow?"

"Of course. I have to defend my man from all those single female vultures."

"Your man, huh?" Dax asked, a smile on his face. He liked how that sounded.

"You are my man, right?"

"And you're my woman," he said definitively. "Oh, one more thing and this one's a doozy."

"I'm ready...Go!"

"My mom and dad will be here tomorrow."

Her mouth dropped. "You're kidding."

"I'm not. I wonder if your mom knows."

"If she does, she didn't tell me. Maybe your mom wants to surprise her." Cori sighed. "It will be a fabulous reunion." She snapped her fingers. "Remember to get Cash off to the side tomorrow and talk to him about Marc's house."

"Yeah, there's something you should know."

"Yeah?"

"Yeah, I'm paying for all the reno as a surprise birthday present for Marc. In fact, and you can't tell him, the ranch is completely paid for."

She looked at him questioningly. "I've heard about millions of dollars sent to foreign places to bribe locals that mysteriously go missing. Am I going to be visiting you in some federal prison?"

He laughed. "No, nothing like that. The friend who died, David Stephens? He was an only child of only children. No heirs, other than tangential relatives many, many times removed from their direct line. David, bless him, left me a nice amount of money to use as I wanted. He wanted me to spend it on me, or however I thought appropriate." He shrugged. "I want to do this for Marc. He would work the rest of his life trying to pay off the mortgage on a ranch like that."

"What about your sister? Think she'll want a house there with y'all? You're planning on building a house there, right?"

"My plan, such as it is, is to buy Sami a house in town. If she wants to live out there, I'm sure we can carve off an area for her, but I expect her to want to be closer to work. As far as my building, it depends on..." He paused. How did he tell her it depended on her—what she wanted? What if what he wanted wasn't what she wanted? What if she needed to stay in town and not in a more rural part of the county?

"Depends on?"

"Well, I guess it depends on whether I settle here or move on."

She jerked around to face him. "Move on? You're thinking of leaving?"

"No, but who knows what the future holds. I didn't plan on having only one leg either."

She grew very quiet.

"You're lucky," he said. "You know what you want to do with your life. You're helping youths every day with your psychology degree."

"And I hate it," she blurted.

"*What?!?*"

"Do you know why I work with children? Because that's what Greg told me I should do. He left and I still followed the plan *he* had for me. Isn't that crazy? I'm a psychologist who needs a psychologist. I don't hate my patients—nothing like that. I like knowing I'm helping, but I despise being inside all day, every day. I was raised outside. After breakfast, I'd hit the backdoor and be gone all day. Most of the time, I was in the barn or riding horses. Sometimes, I'd hang out at the creek and try to catch fish with my hands. I'd pick flowers and make floral leis or chaplets."

"A what?" Dax interjected.

"Chaplet. You know, the floral wreath that goes around the head."

"Got it."

"Anyway, lately, I've been getting itchy and impatient at work. I want to be outside."

"Well, we'll be outside all day tomorrow, and you'll get your sunshine," he said. "And after tomorrow, we can talk about our future."

"Our future?"

"Or futures," he clarified. He didn't want to think he would try to tell her what her future should be, like that asshole Greg had done. "I'd love to talk about this all night, but all I can think about is your nice, firm mattress."

She giggled. "Yeah? You like my mattress?"

"I like being there with you more."

She stood and held out her hand. "Come on, handsome. Let's make sure that cock of yours still works."

He laughed and they walked to her bedroom, followed closely by Kobi and Beatrice, who'd decided cats and dogs could be friends.

The road leading to the Bar M ranch was bumper-to-bumper traffic as townspeople headed out for the annual Montgomery Memorial Day party. Dax and Cori had gotten when he'd thought was an early start —ten a.m.—only to discover everyone else had had the same idea.

As they pulled into the drive, they were stopped by a worker directing traffic. "Name?" the man asked.

"Dax Cooper and Cori Lambert."

The man made a checkmark on the page. "Proceed forward and tell the next guy that Aaron said to let you through the sawhorses. Have a good day."

Dax rolled forward until a second traffic manager stopped him. He rolled down his window and said, "Aaron says we are to go through the sawhorses."

The guy nodded and moved a couple of wooden sawhorses blocking the drive to the house. As soon as they were through, he moved them back into place and directed the next car toward field parking.

"Ohhh," Cori said. "I think I like being with a Montgomery family member."

Dax chuckled. "Did you used to park in the field?"

"Nope. We rode over on horseback. So much easier and faster."

"This is a new world for me." He shook his head as he slowed for another guy directing traffic at the house. When he gave his name, the man directed Dax toward a side field close to the house where a few other cars were parked.

"Nervous?" she asked.

"How did you know?"

"Because I would be nervous. It's kind of like an unveiling, right?"

He groaned. "Now, I just want to go home."

Lacing their fingers, she said, "Just hold on to me. I'm an old hand at this party. Besides, your parents are here somewhere, right? I can't wait to meet them."

His heart zinged at her words. His parents were here. His mom was finally reconnecting with her family. He'd never understood how she'd maintained radio silence with her brothers. He missed his siblings terribly when they were apart.

They exited the car. Cori held one hand, and Kobi's lead was in the other. His head was beginning to ache from the tension in his neck.

"Dax. Cori," a voice called.

Porchia and Darren hurried toward them.

"So good to see you," Porchia said, hugging Cori.

Dax hesitated, unsure of what to say to Darren.

"Is that any way to greet your long-lost cousin?" Darren asked with a broad grin.

Dax extended his hand, but Darren pulled him in for a hug. He expected to panic from the close encounter, but the dread never came. Instead, he felt calmer.

"So, I understand you've known about this for a while," Dax said.

"Yeah, but we didn't want to frighten Marc away by swarming him with Montgomerys."

"Did you know?" Cori asked Porchia, who shook her head.

"I didn't. Darren told me last night. At first, I was a little peeved at him." She slugged his shoulder. "But I understood. Besides, he knows me. I would have told you as soon as you mentioned Dax."

Cori laughed. "Probably so."

"Come on," Darren said. "Let's head out back. I can't wait to meet my aunt Cora."

Dax saw Marc at a distance, standing under some trees talking with Travis, Cash, and Jason Montgomery. Their stances were friendly. Marc's face was lit with a smile and his occasional laughter carried across the distance.

A country band climbed onto a makeshift stage and the music began. People were everywhere. Dax hated crowds, but he didn't feel crowded. It could have been Cori holding his hand. It could have been related to the outdoor setting. Or it could be because he felt surrounded by family, which was an odd, but welcomed, feeling.

They got some drinks and met up with Magda and Reno, who also greeted Dax with a backslapping hug. He was discovering that the Texas Montgomerys were huggers. He wasn't sure how he felt about all the hugging, but so far, he was handling the it well.

There were so many children running around, they reminded him of ants.

"Are all these kids Montgomerys?" he asked Reno.

Reno and Darren laughed.

"A lot of them are," Darren said and began pointing out and naming all the Montgomery offspring.

"I'll never remember all those names," Dax said with a groan. "Don't you guys know about birth control?"

"In our defense, none of these heathens belong to us," Reno said. "Now, Lane's side of the family can't seem to keep their hands off each other." He looked at Magda who gave him a questioning look. "Er, not that we aren't crazy about our wives and can't wait to get them home and in bed."

Magda slugged his arm. "Geez, I'm so flattered. I'm going to get a beer. Want to come, Cori?"

She looked up at Dax.

"I'll be okay," he said.

"I'll be right back. I promise."

The band finished playing a song, and the lead

singer tapped the microphone. "Hey, y'all. Listen up. Lane and Clint have something they want to say."

He stepped back and the two brothers stepped forward.

"Welcome to Bar M ranch," Lane said loudly into the microphone. "Clint and I, along with our wives, look forward to hosting this every year. I swear, the crowd gets bigger every year too. Of course, some of those kiddos running around belong to our kids." He looked at Clint, who stepped to the microphone.

"This year, we are thrilled to add to our Whispering Springs Montgomery family. As many of you know, Lane and I have a younger sister we haven't seen in a while, but that didn't stop her kids from landing here. We are pleased to welcome Marc Singer, Dax Cooper, and Samantha Cooper officially into the Montgomery clan. Please raise a glass and help us welcome our nephews and niece to Whispering Springs."

A cold bottle tapped Dax's knuckles. He took it from Cori and looked around. Townspeople were lifting their drinks and trying to applaud. He could see Marc on the other side being slapped on the back and warmly greeted by people Dax didn't know. Beside him, Reno, Darren, Porchia, and Magda were cheering and whistling while holding their drinks in the air. Cori cheered with them, before standing on her toes to kiss him.

He looked for Sami or his parents, neither of whom he could find. But there were a lot of people, and it would be easy to overlook them. Still, he'd think if his mother were there, Clint would have mentioned her.

As the noise began to fade, Lane stepped back up to the mic. "Clint and I flipped a coin to see who got to introduce our new kin. He lost." The crowd roared with laughter, until he waved down the noise. "What I meant was, I get to do the honors of welcoming my sister, Cora, and her husband, Lon Cooper, to our little soiree."

Dax's mother stepped from behind a hay bale on the stage and waved. Clint and Lane hugged her at the same time. Dax's vision blurred as he fought back the tears. Cori wrapped her arm around Dax's waist.

"She looks so much like you and Marc," she said. "Or maybe I should say you look like her."

"Let's head that way, okay?" he said. "I want you to meet her." What he didn't say was that he wanted his mother to meet the woman he wanted to marry, even if he hadn't told Cori yet.

"I have a better idea," Cori said. "We should head to the back patio of the house. That's where the older Montgomerys hang out all day. You'll never get through this crowd."

He let her lead the way. She was much more familiar with this scene than he was.

Cori led him up a set of steps to where two women had stood watching the activity on the entertainment stage. "Dax, this is Jackie Montgomery, Lane's wife, and Nadine Montgomery, Clint's wife."

To no one's surprise—certainly not his—both women swooped in for hugs.

"So good to meet you," Nadine said. "Clint is beside himself to have your mother here for a visit."

"Same with Lane," Jackie said. "Good to see you again, Dax."

Dax smiled at the older women. "Nice to meet you, Nadine. Good to see you again, Jackie."

"Dax wanted to see his mom," Cori said. "I suggested they'd probably bring her over here, don't you think?"

Jackie shrugged. "Probably, but who knows? Cori, have you seen your parents today?"

"I haven't. I suppose they're here."

"They are," Jackie said. "They were looking for you."

"I'll keep an eye out for them."

"No need," Nadine said. "They're headed this way."

Cori's parents climbed the steps to the patio. Greetings were followed by another round of hugs.

"Mom, Dad, this is Dax Cooper," Cori said.

"Dax, honey, you don't remember me but I held you when you were only a few days old," Clover said. "In fact, you peed on me."

"Oh, lord, mother," Cori groaned.

Dax laughed. "I promise not to do that again."

Clover laughed.

"Nice to meet you, son," Dale said and shook Dax's hand. "You didn't pee on me."

"Whew," Dax said. "That would've been awkward."

"Clover," a high-pitched voice screamed.

"Cora," Clover yelled and rushed toward Dax's mother.

The two women embraced, rocking side-to-side in each other's arms. Dax's mom was crying, but then, so was Cori's mom. They were talking over each other. Dax doubted either knew what the other was saying, but it didn't matter. It was obvious they were happy to see each other.

"Hey, Dale," Marc said as he joined the group.

"Sheriff Singer," Dale said. "This is quite the day."

Suddenly, Dax was grabbed from behind, arms wrapped around his chest, pinning his arms to his sides. His muscles tensed, and he prepared to fight.

Cori wrapped her fingers around his wrist and leaned forward. "It's your mom," she said. "Your mom," she repeated.

He breathed out and turned. "Mom."

She started crying. "Dax. Honey. Are you doing okay?"

Dax smiled. "I'm wonderful, Mom. I want you to meet Cori Lambert."

"Clover's daughter," she said. "Nice to meet you, Cori. I'm glad you and Dax got to meet each other."

Cori chuckled. "Me too."

"Hi, Mom," Marc said, giving his mother a kiss on the cheek. "I'm glad to see you."

"You too, honey. Thanks for taking in Dax and Sami."

Marc rolled his eyes. "He's been so much work,"

he said, gesturing toward Dax, who answered by laughing.

A feeling of being momentarily out of control sent a wave of anxiety through Dax so powerful he swayed. Kobi pressed herself to Dax's leg, putting herself between Dax and the other people surrounding him. His vision narrowed to pinpoints. His breathing was labored and forced. His heart raced across his chest as though it was being chased. His stomach rolled, shooting a blast of gastric acid up this throat.

Then she was there...Cori taking his hand and leading him out of the crowd of family and to a group of stools in the currently unused outdoor kitchen. She pushed him down onto one of the stools and took his cold-water bottle.

"I'm here," she whispered as she rolled the water bottle along the back of his neck. "I'm here. Hold on to me. I've got you. Take some slow deep breaths."

He put an arm around her waist and pressed the side of his face into her abdomen. His heart slowed marginally. He drew in some deep breaths and blew them out.

"Is he okay?" he heard his mother ask.

"He's fine," Cori said. "We just needed some private time."

He didn't look at his mother. She would know instantly that he was having a panic attack. She'd seen him in one before.

"Good," his mom said quietly. "Good. I'm glad you're here with him."

"Always," Cori said.

Dax heard her words, but he wasn't sure what she meant.

"Can you eat something if I go get it?" Cori asked. "A burger? A hot dog? Beef brisket taco?"

"The taco," Dax said. "Something small."

She kissed his forehead. "I'll be right back."

When she left, Dax clung to Kobi's soft hair. The dog grounded him in the here and now. He was safe. He was with friends and family. Nothing could hurt him.

"Well, Dax Cooper," a low, sexy female voice said. "It's about time I met Cori's new guy."

Dax looked into a pair of cold blue eyes set in the face of a goddess. The woman was stunningly beautiful. He needed no introduction. Cori's sister looked very much like their mother.

"I'm Elsie Belle, Cori's sister."

Dax nodded. "I figured as much. You look a lot like your mom."

"Well, we both wore the Miss Texas crown, so I get that comment a lot. Where's my sister?"

"She'll be right back." Dax was a little embarrassed that Cori was doing a food run for him instead of him doing one for her.

Elsie pulled up a stool and sat close to him. "Imagine my surprise to find out that you are the son of the long-lost Montgomery sister. I haven't met your mother yet, but I'll make a point to. You know, I was almost a Montgomery myself. Travis and I go back a long way. Everyone thought we would marry, but I knew he wasn't over his first wife." She shook her head. "Poor Caroline. She'll always be second in his heart."

"I haven't had the pleasure of meeting Caroline, only Travis, but I'll be sure to give her your regards when I do."

Elsie threw back her head in a laugh. She clutched his arm as though they were close and intimate friends. "I have a question for you."

"Oh?"

"Did my sister hook onto you before she knew you were a Montgomery or after?"

"Excuse me?"

"Well, let's face it. Cori doesn't have the Lambert beauty of my mother. Her love life, such as it is, has been dismal, if you want my opinion of the men she's dated. If you're not serious about her, why don't you move on? She doesn't need the heartbreak of being dumped by another man. And really, she can probably do better than an injured soldier she'll have to take care of the rest of her life."

"How dare you speak about your sister that way," he started, but was cut off by a smoking irate Cori.

"Elsie. Have you lost your mind?" Cori asked, her words bitten out.

"Cori, there you are," Elsie said, her voice as smooth as silk. "I was looking for you."

"You were being rude to the man I..." she looked at Dax and said, "the man I love."

Dax's heart beat loudly in his ears. "I love you too, Cori."

"You do? Seriously?" she asked, her eyes bright with tears.

"Yes, I do. I've known for a while, but I wasn't sure how to tell you."

"Me too," Cori said. "I think I knew you were the one the night we went looking at stars."

He chuckled. "I knew you were the one after the first night when you took no pity on my situation."

"Why the hell would I pity you?" she said. "You are a survivor. A woman has to respect that."

Elsie clapped her hands. "This is fabulous. Dax, you passed my test, unlike that fool Greg."

Cori whirled on her sister. "What are you talking about?"

"Only a man who loved you would defend you like he did."

"And Greg fits into this story, how?" Cori snapped,

Elsie rolled her eyes. "That day you walked in, and I was talking with Greg? I knew you'd never break off the engagement, even though it was obvious to me he was a terrible influence, always telling you what to do, what to think, where you would live, and so forth. That day, I casually suggested that I and our parents, thought that, maybe, you were too young to get married and y'all should wait another year. I may have said some awful things about you too. I wanted him to stand up for you, defend you, and be the man who deserved to be married to my little sister. Instead of handling a potential problem, he ran. You didn't need someone like him in your life." Elsie touched

Dax's shoulder gently. "You need a man who'll defend you, even if it is to your own family. Dax was getting ready to lambast me." She smiled at him. "Thank you for loving my sister as much as I do. Can I give you a kiss?"

Stunned, he nodded and she brushed a soft kiss on his cheek.

"Now, I have to run," Elsie said. "Oscar is supposed to be home tonight. You kids have fun."

She hugged Cori. "I do love you, even when you don't think I do."

With that, Elsie flew down the steps and into the crowd.

The rest of the afternoon was filled with meeting Montgomery after Montgomery. The kids were fascinated by Dax's leg. Olivia Montgomery Landry's son Adam wanted Dax to take it off so he could show it off at school. Dax declined the offer to be this week's "show and tell."

The fireworks were scheduled for ten, but he and Cori never made it. By five, they were in his truck and headed back to her house. He could hardly wait to make love to the woman he had every intention of making his wife.

~

Three Days Later

"Surprise," Dax and his entire family yelled as Marc entered the restaurant.

"Happy birthday, bro," Dax said, slapping Marc on the back. "You're getting to be an old man."

"Ha. You're not that far behind me."

"But I have the love of a good woman to keep me young," Dax replied, pulling Cori tightly against him.

"Happy birthday, Marc," Cori said, and kissed his cheek. "You've got a stack of gifts to open and a bunch of people to talk to, so don't let us keep you."

Marc pointed to his eyes and then to Dax and Cori. "I better not catch you two sneaking out the back door early."

Dax laughed easily, something he found himself doing more and more since arriving in Texas. Was it being with his brother and sister again? Or was it the joy of having his mother reunited with her family? He suspected neither of those.

He put all his emotional healing on Cori and her Texan touch.

Later tonight, he and Cori would give Marc his present, a fake deed to the Hanson Ranch showing it paid in full. Until then, he stood with the love of his life and enjoyed the living. Not too many people almost die and get a second chance. He had his second chance at life and he was holding on to it with both hands.

A Note From Cynthia

Thank you for reading A Texan's Touch.

If I haven't told you, I appreciate my readers. Without you, I wouldn't be here.

Readers are always asking: What can I do to help you?

My answer is always the same: PLEASE give me an honest review. Every review helps.

Are you curious about the other couples in the story? They each have their own book! They are listed below and available in digital and print.

Texas Bossa Nova

Texas Hustle

Texas Tango

Texas Twist

Wondering about Marc Singer? Look for **Texas Bombshell** later in 2023.

Check out the Also By for a list of all Cynthia's Books.

THANK YOU again for all your support.

Cynthia

About the Author

 New York Times and USA Today Bestselling author Cynthia D'Alba started writing on a challenge from her husband in 2006 and discovered having imaginary sex with lots of hunky men was fun. She was born and raised in a small Arkansas town. After being gone for a number of years, she's thrilled to be making her home back in Arkansas living in a vine-covered cottage on the banks of an eight-thousand acre lake. When she's not reading or writing or plotting, she's doorman for her border collie, cook, housekeeper and chief bottle washer for her husband and slave to a noisy, messy parrot. She loves to chat online with friends and fans.

You can find her most days at one of the following online homes:

Website: cynthiadalba.com

Facebook:Facebook/cynthiadalba

Twitter:@cynthiadalba

Newsletter:Newsletter Sign-Up

Or drop her a line at cynthiadalba@gmail.com

Or send snail mail to: Cynthia D'Alba PO Box 2116
Hot Springs, AR 71914

Other Books by Cynthia D'Alba

WHISPERING SPRINGS, TEXAS
Texas Two Step – The Prequel
Texas Two Step
Texas Tango
Texas Fandango
Texas Twist
Texas Hustle
Texas Bossa Nova
Texas Lullaby
Saddles and Soot
Texas Daze
A Texan's Touch
Texas Bombshell
Whispering Springs, Texas Volume One
Whispering Springs, Texas Volume Two
Whispering Springs, Texas Volume Three

DIAMOND LAKES, TEXAS
A Cowboy's Seduction
Hot SEAL, Cold Beer
Cadillac Cowboy
Texas Justice
Something's Burning

DALLAS DEBUTANTES
McCool Family Trilogy/Grizzly Bitterroot Ranch Crossover
Hot SEAL, Black Coffee
Christmas in His Arms

Snowy Montana Nights
Hot SEAL, Sweet and Spicy
Six Days and One Knight

Carmichael Family Triplets Trilogy (coming soon)
Hot Assets
Hot Ex
Hot Briefs

SEALs in Paradise
Hot SEAL, Alaskan Nights
Hot SEAL, Confirmed Bachelor
Hot SEAL, Secret Service
Hot SEAL, Labor Day
Hot SEAL, Girl Crush

Mason Security
Her Bodyguard
His Bodyguard
Mason Security Duet

Other Books
Backstage Pass

Texas Two Steps

WHISPERING SPRINGS, TEXAS BOOK 1
©2012 CYNTHIA D'ALBA

Secrets are little time-bombs just waiting to explode.

After six years and too much self-recrimination, rancher Mitch Landry admits he was wrong. He left Olivia Montgomery. Now he'll do whatever it take to convince Olivia to give him a second chance.

Olivia Montgomery survived the break-up with the love of her life. She's rebuilt her life around her business and the son she loves more than life itself. She's not proud of the mistakes she's made—particularly the secret she's kept—but when life serves up manure, you use it to mold yourself into something better.

At a hot, muggy Dallas wedding, they reconnect, and now she's left trying to protect the secret she's held on to for all these years.

Texas Tango

WHISPERING SPRINGS, TEXAS, BOOK 2 ©
2013 CYNTHIA D'ALBA

Sex in a faux marriage can make things oh so real.

Dr. Caroline Graham is happy with her nomadic lifestyle fulfilling short-term medical contracts. No emotional commitments, no disappointments. She's always the one to walk away, never the one left behind. But now her grandmother is on her deathbed, more concerned about Caroline's lack of a husband than her own demise. What's the harm in a little white lie? If a wedding will give her grandmother peace, then a wedding she shall have.

Widower Travis Montgomery devotes his days to building the ranch he and his late wife planned before he lost her to breast cancer. The last piece of acreage he needs is controlled by a lady with a pesky need of her own. Do her a favor and he can have the land. She needs a quick, temporary, faux marriage in exchange for the acreage.

It's a total win-win situation until events begin to snowball and they find, instead of playacting, they've put their hearts at risk.

Texas Fandango

WHISPERING SPRINGS, TEXAS BOOK 3 ©
2014 CYNTHIA D'ALBA

Two-weeks on the beach can deepened more than tans.

Attorney KC Montgomery has loved family friend Drake Gentry forever, but she never seemed to be on his radar. When Drake's girlfriend dumps him, leaving him with two all-expenses paid tickets to the Sand Castle Resort in the Caribbean, KC seizes the chance and makes him an offer impossible to refuse: two weeks of food, fun, sand, and sex with no strings attached.

University Professor Drake Gentry has noticed his best friend's cousin for years, but KC has always been hands-off, until today. Unable to resist, he agrees to her two-week, no-strings affair.

The vacation more than fulfills both their fantasies. The sun is hot but the sex hotter.

Texas Twist

WHISPERING SPRINGS, TEXAS BOOK 4 ©
2014 CYNTHIA D'ALBA

Real bad boys can grow up to be real good men.

Paige Ryan lost everything important in her life. She moves to Whispering Springs, Texas to be near her step-brother. But just as her life is derailed again when the last man in the world she wants to see again moves into her house.

Cash Montgomery is on the cusp of having it all. When a bad bull ride leaves him injured and angry, his only comfort is found at the bottom of a bottle. His family drags him home to Whispering Springs, Texas. With nowhere to go, he moves temporarily into an old ranch house on his brother's property surprised the place is occupied.

The best idea is to move on but sometimes taking the first step out the door is the hardest one.

Loving a bull rider is dangerous, so is falling for him a second time is crazy?

Texas Bossa Nova

WHISPERING SPRINGS, TEXAS BOOK 5
©2014 CYNTHIA D'ALBA

A heavy snowstorm can produce a lot of heat

Magda Hobbs loves being a ranch housekeeper. The job keeps her close to her recently discovered father, foreman at the same ranch. She is immune to all the cowboy charms, except for one certain cowboy, who is wreaking havoc on her libido.

Reno Montgomery is determined to make his fledging cattle ranch a success. Dates with Magda Hobbs rocks his world and then she disappears, leaving him confused and angry. He's shocked when he learns the new live-in housekeeper is Magda Hobbs.

When a freak snowstorm cuts off the outside world, the isolation rekindles their desire. But when the weather and the roads clear, Reno has to work hard and fast to keep the woman of his dreams from hitting the road right out of his life again.

Texas Hustle

WHISPERING SPRINGS, TEXAS BOOK 6
©2015 CYNTHIA D'ALBA

Watch out for chigger bites, love bites and secrets that bite

Born into a wealthy, Southern family, Porchia Summers builds a good life in Texas until a bad news ex-boyfriend tracks her down. Desperate for time to figure out how to handle the trouble he brings, she looks to the one man who can get her out of town for a few days.

Darren Montgomery has had his eye on the town's sexy, sweet baker for a while but she's never returns his looks until now. He's flattered but suspicious about her quick change in attention.

Sometimes, camping isn't just camping. It's survival.

Texas Lullaby

WHISPERING SPRINGS, TEXAS BOOK 7
©2016 CYNTHIA D'ALBA

Sometimes what you think you don't want is exactly what you need.

After a long four-year engagement, Lydia Henson makes her decision. Forced to choice between having a family or marrying a man who adamantly against fathering children, she chooses the man. She can live without children. She can't live without the man she loves.

Jason Montgomery doesn't want a family, or at least that's his story and he's sticking to it. The falsehood is less emasculating than the truth.

On the eve of their wedding, Jason and Lydia's well-planned life is thrown into chaos. Everything Jason has sworn he doesn't want is within his grasp. But as he reaches for the golden ring, life delivers another twist.

Saddles and Soot

WHISPERING SPRINGS, TEXAS BOOK 8
©2015 CYNTHIA D'ALBA

Veterinarian Georgina Greyson will only be in Whispering Springs for three months. She isn't looking for love or roots, but some fun with a hunky fireman could help pass the time.

Tanner Marshall loves being a volunteer fireman, maybe more than being a cowboy. At thirty-four, he's ready to put down some roots, including marriage, children and the white picket fence.

When Georgina accidentally sets her yard on fire during a burn ban, the volunteer fire department responds. Tanner hates carelessness with fire, but there's something about his latest firebug that he can't get out of his mind.

Can an uptight firefighter looking to settle down persuade a cute firebug to give up the road for a house and roots?

Texas Daze

WHISPERING SPRINGS, TEXAS BOOK 9
©2017 CYNTHIA D'ALBA

A quick fling can sure heat up a cowgirl's life

When a devastating discovery ends Marti Jenkins' engagement, she decides to play the field for a while. A ranch accident lands her in the office of Whispering Springs' new orthopedic doctor, Dr. Eli Boone. And yeah, he's as hot as she's been told.

Dr. Eli Boone is temporarily covering his friend's practice and then it's back to New York City and the societal world he's lives. He's not looking for a wife, but he wouldn't say no to a quick tumble in the sheets with the right woman.

Due to ridiculous challenge, Eli has to learn to ride before he leaves town. He turns to the one person who can help him win the bet, Marti Jenkins.

As he learns to ride a horse, Marti does a little riding of her own...and she doesn't need a horse.

Texas Bombshell

WHISPERINGS SPRINGS, TX BOOK 11
(C)2023 CYNTHIA D'ALBA

What happens when fate blows your life to hell?

From NYT and USA Today bestselling author Cynthia D'Alba comes a steamy romance with a hot cowboy, a smart heroine and two meddling mothers who scheme the perfect meet cute.

Sheriff Marc Singer isn't looking to remarry. Widow Dr. Jennifer Tate is focused on her career and raising her genius daughter. Thrown together sixteen years after their divorce, Marc and Jenn must face the reality that one night of passion after their divorce left them with a lifelong connect. Will they find that time heals all wounds and give themselves a second chance? Can a divorced couple go home again?

If you like relatable heroes, plenty of wit and charm, and small-town backdrops, you'll adore Cynthia D'Alba's tale of beginning all over again. Tap the link to buy the book today!